S0-ADP-137

"**I guess I should apologize for insinuating that you're a two-timing snake,**" Elissa whispered.

Without knowing quite how it happened, she was in his arms, pressed against him so tightly she could feel every plane of his body.

Gray felt exhilaration surge through him. He tried to remember the last time he'd felt so alive. "I'm waiting for that apology," he said huskily.

Her arms crept up around his neck and her body arched into his. "Do you want it in words?" she murmured. Her lips curved into a slow, sexy smile. "Or in actions?"

He gazed into her laughing, challenging eyes and was lost. All his efforts to keep away from her, the walls he'd built to keep her out, were swept away in a tidal wave of need. He'd wanted her from the moment he'd seen her, a hunger that would not be denied.

His mouth came down on hers, hard and hot. A shudder of desire racked him. "You make me crazy," he said hoarsely, gliding his hands over Elissa's body.

She looked at him with glowing eyes, her lipstick thoroughly kissed away. "It's only fair," she said. "You started making me crazy a long time ago. . . ."

WHAT ARE *LOVESWEPT* ROMANCES?

They are stories of true romance and touching emotion. We believe those two very important ingredients are constant in our highly sensual and very believable stories in the *LOVESWEPT* line. Our goal is to give you, the reader, stories of consistently high quality that may sometimes make you laugh, sometimes make you cry, but are always fresh and creative and contain many delightful surprises within their pages.

Most romance fans read an enormous number of books. Those they truly love, they keep. Others may be traded with friends and soon forgotten. We hope that each *LOVESWEPT* romance will be a treasure—a "keeper." We will always try to publish

LOVE STORIES YOU'LL NEVER FORGET
BY AUTHORS YOU'LL ALWAYS REMEMBER

The Editors

582

Barbara Boswell
Private Lessons

BANTAM BOOKS
NEW YORK · TORONTO · LONDON · SYDNEY · AUCKLAND

PRIVATE LESSONS

A Bantam Book / December 1992

*LOVESWEPT® and the wave design are registered
trademarks of Bantam Books, a division of
Bantam Doubleday Dell Publishing Group, Inc.
Registered in U.S. Patent
and Trademark Office and elsewhere.*

*All rights reserved.
Copyright © 1992 by Barbara Boswell.
Cover art copyright © 1992 by Garin Baker.
No part of this book may be reproduced or transmitted
in any form or by any means, electronic or mechanical,
including photocopying, recording, or by any
information storage and retrieval system, without
permission in writing from the publisher.
For information address: Bantam Books.*

*If you purchased this book without a cover you should be
aware that this book is stolen property. It was reported as
"unsold and destroyed" to the publisher and neither the
author nor the publisher has received any payment for this
"stripped book."*

*If you would be interested in receiving protective vinyl
covers for your Loveswept books, please write to this address
for information:*

*Loveswept
Bantam Books
P.O. Box 985
Hicksville, NY 11802*

ISBN 0-553-44311-9

Published simultaneously in the United States and Canada

*Bantam Books are published by Bantam Books, a division of
Bantam Doubleday Dell Publishing Group, Inc. Its trademark,
consisting of the words "Bantam Books" and the portrayal of
a rooster, is Registered in U.S. Patent and Trademark Office
and in other countries. Marca Registrada. Bantam Books, 666
Fifth Avenue, New York, New York 10103.*

PRINTED IN THE UNITED STATES OF AMERICA

OPM   0 9 8 7 6 5 4 3 2 1

One

He felt tense and restless; he'd been feeling that way all day. So Gray McCall sought relief with what he knew was a sure cure. As a man of action, his antidote to anything—be it frustration, exasperation, worry, anger, grief, or even this vague tension that gripped him—was exercise. Strenuous, sweat-inducing, pulse-pounding, thought-blocking exercise.

Dressed in shorts, running shoes, and a T-shirt, he pulled his car into the Riverview Junior High School parking lot and climbed out. Some nights he ran around the track there until he thought he would collapse. Then he would drag himself back to his car and drive along the quiet country road that led to the tract of condominiums where he lived, on the outskirts of the small Ohio town of Riverview. After a warm shower he'd fall into bed, too exhausted to move or think.

It was past seven, but the sky was still light, and the warm September evening felt more like summer than the "school night" it actually was. The neighborhood kids seemed to feel the same way. Gray noticed a group of them playing in the grassy field as he walked toward the track that surrounded it.

2 • BARBARA BOSWELL

"Aaron, Aaron, kick it to Bobby! He'll kick it in."

Kick. Gray's ears perked. That was a soccer term. As coach of Riverview Senior High School's boys' soccer team, he was ever attuned to anything having to do with soccer. But he was surprised to hear what was clearly a female voice calling the play. Younger girls and boys played soccer together, but these youngsters appeared to be of junior high school age, a time when the sexes were usually segregated, sportswise at least.

Walking closer, he saw the boys running in fast pursuit of a soccer ball. A girl—no, a woman—was running alongside, shouting instructions to them in coachlike fashion.

A boy kicked the ball toward the goal, and the goalkeeper made a spectacular leaping kick, sending the ball flying off the field. A loud mix of cheers and boos broke the evening quiet, followed by a furious harangue from several of the boys.

"Why didn't you kick it to Bobby, stupid?"

"Aaron, you're always trying to be a hero, but you always lose."

"If Aaron's on my team next time, I'm not playing!"

The woman who'd called the play interrupted them. "Come on, guys," she said. "Give Aaron a break. He was trying his best."

Gray recognized some of the players from the junior soccer camp program he ran for a month each summer. One of the boys, the object of the others' scorn, was twelve-year-old Aaron Emory, youngest brother of Seth Emory, a senior and one of the star players on the high school soccer team.

"Anyway, it's just a game, guys," the woman went on, her tone clear and logical, with a hint of coaxing. "Who cares who wins or loses? We're just playing for fun."

Well familiar with the psyche of young males, Gray knew her approach wasn't going to work even before the boys started hooting.

He frowned, suddenly realizing he knew the woman. She was Elissa Emory, older sister of Seth and Aaron, and one of his former students. She had returned to Riverview High that term to teach art while the school's regular art teacher was on sabbatical.

What was an art teacher, he wondered, and a female one at that, doing clutching a soccer ball, surrounded by a swarm of shouting, bellicose kids?

His curiosity roused, he walked nearer, his gaze sweeping over her. A different image rose in his mind, an image of the high school cheerleader she'd been eight years ago—a cute teenager with big blue eyes and an engaging, irresistible smile, a bubbly kid whose expressive face conveyed her every emotion. She had taken one of the biology courses he taught, and though she hadn't been one of his better students, she'd certainly been a memorable one. She had kept him amused and entertained, though she'd possessed an astonishing capacity to madden him at times as well.

That bubbly, cute kid was no more, however. Elissa Emory had grown into a woman who fully qualified for the descriptive old term "knockout." Her pale blue eyes, fringed by thick dark lashes and framed by perfectly sculpted dark brows, had always been striking. Now, he saw, they packed an awesome wallop.

She had a smooth ivory complexion, high cheekbones, and a cupid's bow mouth. Her thick ash-blond hair was cut in a sleek bob, angling from a wedge at her nape to swing into a curve just below her chin. Long bangs fell over her forehead, emphasizing her delicate features and giving her a sultry, exotic look.

Her slender, almost boyish high school figure had undergone some transformations, too. She was still slender, but she was also enticingly rounded in all the right places. Her breasts were full and mature, her hips smoothly curved. Gray felt an odd, unwelcome tightening in his middle. It was definitely time for him to start running until he dropped!

"Hey, Coach McCall!" One of the kids spotted him and motioned him over.

He reluctantly postponed his run and joined the group.

"Did you see my brother Andrew's block?" Aaron Emory asked, beaming with brotherly pride. "Is he the best goalkeeper you ever saw, or what?"

"It was a good play," Gray agreed. Thirteen-year-old Andrew had been the goalkeeper whose incredible kick had blocked the goal—and led to his kid brother's humiliation. Young Aaron didn't seem to care, however.

Others did. "If you saw that play, then you also saw Aaron the Idiot lose the game for us," said a disgruntled teammate. He scowled at Aaron. "You were supposed to let Bobby kick it in, jerkface."

"That's enough, Dennis," Elissa said firmly, moving to stand eyeball-to-eyeball with the boy. The fact that he was two inches taller and a lot heavier than she didn't seem to faze her in the least. "Name-calling and fighting don't belong in soccer or in any other game."

"Except maybe hockey," one of the boys suggested.

"Including hockey," she said. "So if you're going to be a poor sport, Dennis, then you—"

"You can't tell me I can't play!" Dennis shouted, cutting her off in mid-sentence. He turned around, sending an appeal to Gray. "She can't, can she, Coach McCall?"

"I didn't hear her say that," Gray said calmly. "You interrupted her before she had a chance to finish speaking. Now, as an impartial observer here, I'd say you owe Aaron an apology, Dennis."

He launched into a quick, friendly pep talk about good sportsmanship, then went into the virtues of team-playing. "That means not going for the glory yourself, but putting the team first, Aaron," he added. "Like when Elissa told you to let Bobby kick the ball in. That was a good call for the team and you should've listened to her."

Aaron nodded his understanding. Dennis said he was sorry. Gray had the two boys shake hands. "Okay." He patted their shoulders. "Now, all of you, get back out there on the field and let's see what you can do."

Automatically he took the ball from Elissa, dropped it to the ground, and gave it a hard, swift kick. The ball fairly flew across the field, and the boys yelled their admiration at its speed and distance as they went running off to play.

Gray and Elissa were left standing alone. It occurred to him that this was the first time they'd had an opportunity to talk since her return to Riverview. With his biology classroom and lab on the third floor of the high school and the art room in the basement, their paths simply didn't cross. He'd seen her around, at soccer games when she'd come to watch her brother Seth play, and at the occasional faculty meeting, but they never seemed to be within speaking distance.

Now they stood in silence, watching the boys play. Gray kept sneaking surreptitious glances at her, and he became aware of a strange tension building in her. She kept shifting her feet, crossing her arms and then uncrossing them, shoving her hands into the pockets of her shorts. If he hadn't remembered what a self-confident, outspoken teenager she'd been, he would think she was nervous. He was about to speak, when she did.

"I guess I should thank you," she said, "for stepping in and handling the situation with the boys."

Her tone implied that she really wasn't thanking him at all. He stared at her curiously, wondering at the slight edge in her voice. Unfortunately as he stared, his gaze drifted down over her body, over her lightly tanned legs. His eyes widened and he forced his gaze back up, focusing on the white sweatband that held her damp hair off her face. That was safe enough to look at.

He cleared his throat. "Uh, sorry. I didn't mean to butt in and take over like that."

She lifted her chin a fraction higher. "Yes, you did."

He fought a smile. "Okay, maybe I did. I didn't like seeing a minor incident blown out of proportion by an overprotective older sister."

She turned to face him, hands on her hips. "I'm not overprotective. But I had to say something. Those boys are always picking on my poor little brother, just because he's smaller than they are and doesn't play quite as well. Aaron tries so hard, but they call him names and criticize him and—"

"Kids that age insult each other all the time. It's almost a ritual with them. You wouldn't have done Aaron a favor by breaking up the game because one of the boys called him a name, Elissa."

"I wasn't going to do that!"

"But you were going to kick Dennis out of the game."

"Well, yes," she admitted. "But he deserved it. You heard the things he said to Aaron, didn't you? And he's been behaving like that all night, toward everyone. Don't you ever discipline your players, *Coach McCall?*"

Her sarcastic inflection amused him, but he again held back his smile, sensing she was not similarly amused. "Of course I do. But there's a crucial difference, Elissa. I'm the coach of the team. These kids playing here tonight are not an organized team, and you're not their coach. You're Aaron's older sister."

"And interference from his big sister will only lead to his being further ridiculed." She sighed. "I know that, of course, but I just can't stand by and let him be bullied. That's the main reason why I came over here with the boys tonight. I wanted to keep an eye on things. On Aaron, in particular."

She looked up sharply, her eyes filled with concern. "You don't think I made matters worse by being here, do you?"

She had the most beautiful eyes he'd ever seen. For several seconds Gray could only stare into them, feeling oddly disoriented. "No," he said slowly, dragging his gaze from her. He forced himself to focus on the boys racing across the field. "But I admit it's a tricky path to walk, the fine line between guidance and interference."

"It's more like walking a tightrope," she said, grimacing. "Without a safety net."

He nodded. "It's tough. Boys that age are notoriously rough on each other."

"But is it too much to expect them to behave like human beings?" she said, her voice rising. "To show some patience and understanding and compassion to a twelve-year-old kid whose whole world has been turned upside down because some drunk driver—"

She broke off, her lips tightening, but Gray knew what she had been about to say. Because some drunk driver who had run a red light had plowed into her mother's car three months earlier, gravely injuring her. Seth had told him about it during summer practice, and Gray knew Mrs. Emory was still at the Lincoln Park Rehabilitation Hospital, relearning how to do the most basic of tasks.

He watched Elissa. She was rubbing her bare arms and rocking back and forth, in constant motion, an obvious clue that she was tense and wired. "Calm down," he said softly. "It's over now and everything is all right. The kids are—"

"Look at that!" She suddenly pointed to the field. "That tall blond kid, the one who looks like a Nazi stormtrooper—I think his name's Jesse—he just deliberately tripped Aaron. This has got to stop right now." Impulsively she started toward the players.

Quick as a flash Gray caught her around the waist with one arm and held her in place. "Penalty!" he shouted in such a dominant, commanding voice, no player dared to question him. "Against Jesse. The other side gets a penalty kick."

Jesse and the others accepted the verdict without protest.

"Let me go!" Elissa said, wiggling in his grasp.

He held her fast. "Look, Elissa, I know you mean well, but you can't fight Aaron's battles for him. If you try, you'll only make things worse for him. It's best just to stay out of it."

"That's easy for you to say. You're not at home with him, seeing a boy who used to be happy and confident turn into a quiet, sad kid who doesn't believe he can do anything right. Sometimes I hear him crying in his room—" Again, she cut herself off. "I shouldn't have said that. Aaron would die if he knew I'd told anybody that, especially you, River-view's most exalted coach."

"The secret's safe with me," Gray said. "I can certainly understand a young boy missing his mother. I lost both my parents in a plane crash when I was only a few years older than Aaron."

Now, why had he blurted that out? Gray wondered. He never talked about his parents. He never had, except with his brother, Gordon, and later, Gordon's wife, Jackie. Why on earth had he mentioned them now, on the junior high playing field, and to Elissa Emory? He regretted it immediately and hoped she would let it pass without comment.

She didn't, of course. She turned to him, her eyes mirroring horror and sympathy. "Both your parents were killed when you were that young? That's awful. I didn't know. I—I'm sorry."

He nodded, carefully looking at the boys' game and not at her big, soft eyes. He was vaguely aware that his arm was still around her, that he could feel her body heat through the sweat-damp cotton of her shirt.

"What happened to you?" she went on. "Who did you live with? Where did you go?"

She moved closer to him, unconsciously, he thought, until her hip was lightly touching his thigh. He couldn't resist tightening his arm around her waist.

"My brother and I went to live with our father's aunt." Gray had to smile at the thought of Aunt Kay. "She's sort of an Auntie Mame type, a nonconformist who nevertheless took her responsibility for us very seriously. She even tried to do traditional things like baking cookies, although we ended up pleading with her to buy Oreos instead."

"Was your brother older or younger than you?"

"Older, by three and a half minutes. And he never let me forget it."

"Twins?"

He nodded. "Yeah. Twins."

"Identical?"

"In every way." He grinned, remembering the good old days. "You wouldn't believe the trouble people had telling us apart. We looked more alike than those Kovach twins in this year's sophomore class. There were times we played it to the hilt too."

"So there are actually *two* of you?" she teased in mock horror. "Now, there's a scary thought. Does your twin brother teach impossibly hard biology courses and coach soccer too?"

"No." Gray had no intention of revealing Gordon's fate. He'd long made it a habit not to confide personal information to anyone. He hadn't meant to blurt out the facts of his parents' demise to Elissa, and he would not compound that error by talking about Gordon. It meant too much, hurt too much.

Quickly he sought to turn the conversation away from himself. "Seth told me about your mother's accident. I was sorry to hear it. How is she coming along?"

Elissa sighed. "Slowly. Too slowly for both Mom and Dad. She gets frustrated and cries and wants to give up. Then Daddy gets mad because *he's* so frustrated and worried. He wants her home and everything back to normal so badly. It's—it's—" She paused. "Hard."

"I bet that's an understatement."

She stared at the ground. "It's been especially rough on Aaron and Andrew. They're used to having Mom around all the time and now she's not, and the person that we visit at the rehab hospital . . . Well, she isn't really like the mother they knew."

"Poor kids," Gray said with feeling. "And your poor mother. It's a damn shame." He wished he could think of something more eloquent, more articulate, to express his deep empathy for their situation.

"That's why I'm here," Elissa continued. "I was living in California, but I came home right after the accident and realized that I couldn't go back until Mom was . . . herself again. My dad is hopeless when it comes to cooking and laundry and running a house.

"When I applied to Riverview to work as a substitute teacher, I learned that the art teacher was planning to take a sabbatical for the year. Since I'm an art teacher, I was hired full-time. My friend Connie Ware—"

"The Connie Ware who teaches sophomore English at Riverview? My former general-biology student? That Connie Ware?"

"The one and only. We've been friends since high school and stayed close through the years. Anyway, Connie said the timing was definitely the work of Fate—with a capital letter." Elissa smiled. "Connie's very big on things like Fate and Destiny and Kismet. She talks about them like they were people you might run into on the street."

Gray laughed. "Connie's always been kind of . . . of . . ." He paused, searching for a suitable adjective.

"Of," Elissa repeated, laughing, too. "There's no precise word for her."

"I was amazed when she came back to Riverview as a teacher." He shook his head. "Having her in a classroom was like teaching in a TV sitcom. Now she's in charge of her own class. What a concept!"

"It's sort of like a sequel. How about, 'Connie In Class, Two'? Using Roman numerals of course."

"'The Terror Continues,'" Gray suggested.

They laughed together, warmly, companionably, like two old friends.

Elissa looked up into Gray's dark, dark eyes, and suddenly full awareness of how close they were standing, of the warmth and pressure of his hand on her waist, of how easy it was to confide in him, to laugh with him, surged through her with tidal-wave force. And with that awareness came other more volatile emotions, particularly the memory of the fierce, hopeless passion that Gray McCall had evoked within her eight years ago.

Since returning to Riverview, she had tried but could not forget the mad, mad crush she'd had on him, when she was a seventeen-year-old high school senior and he had been her biology teacher. And hers had been no secret, quiet crush enacted in the privacy of her own mind either. Oh no, that was not her style.

Just thinking back to the way she'd behaved then, following Gray McCall around, flirting with him, talking about him all the time to anyone and everyone, brought a blush to her cheeks. The fact that he had given her no encouragement hadn't held her back one bit. On the contrary, she'd continued her pursuit of him her entire senior year, concocting romantic fantasies about a relationship between them.

It was a relationship that had existed strictly in her schoolgirl imagination. In reality Gray had done nothing to suggest even remotely that he saw her as anything other than one of his students. She certainly understood that now, but back then she'd blindly misinterpreted his every word, look, and gesture to fuel her daydreams.

Her breath caught as she stole a sidelong glance at him. He was thirty-four years old now, in his full masculine prime, about six feet tall and with the trim muscular build of an athlete. His blue running shorts showcased his lean, flat belly and long, powerful thighs; the white cotton shirt displayed his broad, thoroughly masculine chest and shoulders, and those hard, muscled forearms she'd swooned over in high school. Her gaze slid upward, to his thick, dark brown hair, his strong jaw and high cheekbones, his striking black eyes and impossibly sensual mouth.

There was one thing she couldn't fault her adolescent self for, and that was her taste in men. Gray McCall was a vital, sexy man, even more attractive now than he had been eight years ago.

She flushed at that unnerving realization. Suddenly aware that she'd drifted into an intimate scrutiny of the man, she dragged her gaze away from him. No, she vowed fiercely. She was not going to flip over him again! She was a mature woman of twenty-five, the dependable, reliable mainstay of her family, not a giddy schoolgirl.

"So anyway," she said, forcing her voice to be cool and dismissive, "that's why I'm back in Riverview." She slipped free of his arm and swiftly moved away.

Her abrupt withdrawal bothered Gray, more than it should have. He resented the loss of the camaraderie that had been developing between them, though he wasn't sure why he should. But as he gazed at her standing a few feet away with her back to him, and as he felt his heart pound harder and his breathing quicken in the unmistakable signs of burgeoning sexual excitement, he understood. No, Elissa Emory wasn't a bubbly teenager anymore; she was an intriguing woman whom he wanted to get to know. He started toward her, grinning as he wondered if her unexpected coolness was because she'd just remembered that she had nearly flunked his biology course. He shook his head. She had to be the worst biology student he'd ever had.

He had just reached her when she exclaimed, "Oh, my God." She whirled to face him, looked momentarily startled that he was so close, then pointed toward the field. "Look, Aaron's bleeding! There's blood all over his face! That does it! This time they've gone too far!"

She started toward the boys, but only made it about two and a half feet before Gray caught her again, this time wrapping both arms around her waist and spinning her around in the opposite direction.

"Let me go!" she demanded. "I have to help my—"

"Let me handle this, Elissa."

"No! Stop interfering. Aaron is my baby brother and—"

"I'm not interfering. These kids will probably be playing soccer for me in a few years, and I'll also have the redoubtable task of trying to teach them biology as well, so that gives me a vested interest in their future. You're too emotionally involved to do any good, Elissa. Just stay here and keep out of this."

He released her and strode toward the boys.

Elissa was incredulous. Did he actually believe she would stand meekly aside and obey him? "Try and make me," she said, and started running.

They raced each other to where the boys were crowded in a huddle. Gray muscled his way into the group, Elissa right behind him.

"We bumped heads," Aaron said sheepishly, trying

to stem the blood flowing from his nose. "I think Bobby is worse off than me."

A quick glance confirmed that Bobby was indeed in similar or worse straits, trying to blot the blood from his nose with his shirt. Elissa dug into the pocket of her shorts and pulled out some tissues at the same moment that Gray removed a handkerchief from his pocket. They handed both to the boys.

"You do have a head as hard as concrete, kid," Elissa said, rumpling Aaron's hair. She was so relieved it was a simple accident. "Poor Bobby." She tousled his hair, too.

The boys laughed.

"I think it's time to call it a night," Gray said, glancing at his watch. "It's almost dark and Bobby and Aaron need to get home to apply cold packs. Anybody need a ride?"

"I do," Bobby said. "I live about four blocks from here. The Emorys do, too. They live across the street from me."

"We can walk," Elissa said quickly.

"Not me," Aaron said. "I want to ride home with Coach McCall. My nose is bleeding too much to walk."

"Okay, you go with him," Elissa said. "Andrew and I will walk home. Get the ball, Andrew, and let's go."

Andrew glanced from Gray to Elissa. "I want to ride home with them, too, Lissy." He looked at Gray in admiration. "Seth says you have a Jeep Cherokee, Coach McCall. Way cool! I'd like to ride in it."

"Sure," Gray said easily. He started toward the parking lot, the three boys following him. They'd gone a few yards when he paused and turned. "Are you sure you don't want a ride, Elissa?"

"Absolutely," she called back.

Gray pondered whether or not to force the issue. Though Riverview's crime rate was almost negligible, the idea of a woman walking alone in the dusky darkness evoked a certain apprehension. Should he go back and insist that she come with them?

"Try and make me." Her earlier challenge echoed in his head. What if he did just that? His lips twisted into a grim smile. What a bloodbath that would be. Elissa Emory had a mind of her own, and heaven help the unfortunate man who tried to make her do anything she didn't care to do.

"Be careful," he felt obliged to call out anyway.

Elissa made no reply. She was already out of sight.

Two

Elissa knew a shortcut through the neighborhood and arrived home several minutes before she heard Gray's vehicle pull up in front of the house.

She was waiting in the kitchen with a cold dish towel for Aaron's nose when the boys trooped in, followed by Gray McCall himself. "You don't have to stay," she said. "I can take care of Aaron myself."

"I'm sure you can," Gray said. "But I thought if you needed anything, I—"

"We don't," she assured him. "Thanks for bringing the boys home, and good night."

"Elissa, that's kind of rude," Andrew admonished her. He took it upon himself to make up for her breach of hospitality. "Coach McCall, do you want something to drink? Like a cola?" His voice lowered conspiratorially. "Or how about a beer? My dad keeps some in the refrigerator in the basement. Four different brands." He proceeded to rattle off the names.

Something in his tone alarmed Elissa. She pictured Andrew and his friends skulking around the basement, taking inventory of all that available beer. It was definitely time to squelch whatever plans might be in the making. "If you or your friends ever try to sample any of that beer, Andrew," she said sternly, "I'll make sure that you're grounded until you graduate from high school. And don't think that I won't or can't."

Andrew's face flushed dark red and he stared at the floor.

Gray felt sorry for him. He was obviously humiliated by his big sister's threat after his attempt to be manly. Gray knew all about young boys' fragile egos. "Hey, I'll take a cola, Andrew. Thanks for offering," he added.

Brightening, Andrew went to the refrigerator.

"Did you have to come down so hard on the kid?" Gray murmured to Elissa in a low voice, as she placed the wet rag on Aaron's nose. "He was only trying to—"

"He was showing off," she countered. "I don't happen to think it's cute for an eighth-grader to be running around offering beer to people. Our mother was badly hurt by a drunk driver, and I have no—"

"Not that lecture again!" Andrew said. His face was beet-red as he handed the opened can of soda to Gray. "I'll never drive drunk, Elissa. I know what happened to Mom. But I wish—I just wish you'd shut up about it sometimes!" He ran from the room.

"I'll go talk to him," Aaron said. "Don't worry, Elissa, he's just in one of his moods." The younger boy patted his sister's arm, then left the kitchen, still clutching the cloth to his nose.

Elissa and Gray were left alone. Her shoulders slumped. "Go ahead and say it," she muttered in a tired, defeated voice. "I overreacted."

From the corner a yellow canary in a spacious two-tiered bird cage emitted a series of emphatic chirps. Elissa sighed. "Even Peep agrees."

Gray glanced at the noisy bird, then back at Elissa. "Peep is being overly critical, I think. Try to look at the situation the way I used to view the results of your biology experiments. You tried, but you blew it."

"I know." She sank down onto a kitchen chair. "These days I can't do anything right in Andrew's eyes. I wish Seth were around more. Andrew just idolizes him."

"What about your dad?" Gray sat down in the chair opposite hers. "Where's he?"

"Daddy is an air traffic controller in Columbus, and he works different shifts, sometimes even double shifts depending on the airport's schedules and needs." She traced a pattern on the surface of the Formica table, keeping her eyes averted from him. "And since Mom's accident, Daddy hasn't been himself. He's so worried and preoccupied that he hasn't been able to give much attention to the kids."

"So in effect, you've been both mother and father to the boys."

"Kind of." She sighed heavily. "Maybe if they were girls, it would be easier, because I sure don't seem to know what makes boys that age tick. It's hard to be interested in the things that interest them, sports and Nintendo and stuff like that." She smiled wryly. "Now, if they wanted to talk nail polish or hair styles or whether hemlines are going up or down, I'd be right on target."

"True. But if they were interested in wearing nail polish or skirts, you'd have a whole new set of problems."

She laughed, feeling cheered in spite of the fact that nothing had really changed. Somehow Gray had known exactly the right thing to say to draw her out of all that threatening angst. Elissa had never been one for soul-wrenching angst. She much preferred action—and humor.

"Good point," she said, grinning at him.

Gray's breath caught in his throat. The dimples in her cheeks were enchanting; her blue eyes sparkled with laughter. And her mouth . . . He gulped. Her lips looked soft and pink and sensually full. Tempting, so excitingly, alarmingly tempting . . .

He quickly dragged his gaze away. This wasn't happening, he assured himself, even as the blood pulsed hotly through his veins. He wasn't really feeling this breathtaking dizziness as he stared at her. His body wasn't becoming hot and hard and—

He jumped to his feet. It was an illusion, he swore to himself. All of it. These thoughts, these *feelings*, they weren't real. He refused to let them be real. He'd had it with the searing ups and downs of volatile emotions. At long last his life was calm and predictable, exactly as he wanted it, and he had no intention of allowing anything, or anyone, disturb his hard-won peace. And if anyone could, every self-protective instinct he possessed warned him, it would be *her*, Elissa Emory.

"Look, I've got to go." Without a backward glance or another word, he bolted from the kitchen like someone fleeing a leaking nuclear reactor site.

Elissa blinked. "What was that all about?" she asked aloud.

Peep replied with a melodic warble.

Elissa chewed her lower lip thoughtfully, reviewing the scene in her mind. They'd been talking, laughing, she'd looked at him and . . .

This time she jumped to her feet, so fast she almost overturned the chair. *How* had she been looking at him? she wondered, her heart beginning to pound heavily. Had something in the way she'd looked reminded him of her long-ago pursuit of him? Was he worried that she had misinterpreted his friendliness, that she'd taken his presence in her kitchen as encouragement to begin the chase all over again?

Elissa's whole body blushed. He was wrong, of course, but he didn't know that. He'd run out like he was barely escaping with his life. Because he believed he was escaping the clutches of an infatuated, relentless Elissa Emory? She felt a crashing wave of humiliation, what she always experienced when she thought back to how young and foolish she'd been.

"You don't have to worry, Coach," she said, wishing he could hear. "I am not going to inflict myself on you again, not in any way, shape, or form. I'll stay out of your way, that's a promise."

The next evening, in a small frame house in the town of Blairsville, a few miles south of Riverview, Gray sat at the kitchen table with a screwdriver, attaching a small wheel to a doll-sized dune buggy. Across the kitchen a tall, attractive woman scooped generous portions of salad from a large ceramic bowl into three smaller ones.

"Mandy sounds even more excited about her dance class this year than last," Gray said, smiling at the woman. "And after seeing her dance recital in June, I think the kid definitely has talent, Jackie."

Jackie grimaced wryly. "I wish she were as enthusiastic about her schoolwork as she is about her dancing and her gymnastics and her dolls and her—"

"Hey, that's my niece you're talking about," Gray cut in good-humoredly. "She's only eight and she happens to be perfect, you know."

Jackie laughed. "I know *you* think so." She set the salad bowls on the table and began to heap spaghetti onto three dinner plates. "Can you stand spaghetti again? I seem to make it three times a week, but it's quick and easy."

"I love your spaghetti," Gray said. "Hey, Jackie, eating at your house is like dining at a four-star restaurant, no matter what you serve."

"That's only in comparison to your own cooking," she teased. "I've often wondered how a smart guy like you finds cooking so completely unlearnable."

"I think it's in the genes. Gordon couldn't get the hang of boiling water either, remember?"

Jackie gazed off into space. "I remember," she said quietly.

There was a brief silence, then she went on. "Gray, Paul asked me to marry him last night." She ladled meatballs and sauce over the spaghetti, her gaze darting from her task to Gray, who sat silent and still at the table. "I haven't told Mandy or my parents yet. I wanted you to be the first to know."

Gray took a deep breath, then stood and crossed the kitchen to put his arm around her. "I'm happy for you, Jackie. Paul's a great guy." He hugged her tighter. "And I hope he knows what a lucky guy he is, getting you and Mandy. In any case, I intend to tell him so."

He turned her in his arms and gazed down at her. "I hope you're not worried about me or my reaction, Jackie. I understand that the past is gone, and I really want you to be happy. You're too young and too loving to spend your life alone." Dark memories flashed through him, but he pressed on. "And it'll be great for Mandy to be part of a new family. I take it you and Paul intend to have kids of your own?"

Jackie nodded. "We'd like that very much. Gray, I just want you to know that I really loved Gordon and—and I always will."

"I know that, Jackie. You were everything a wife could be to him. I don't know how he could've handled . . . everything without you there beside him every step of the way. I don't know how I would've managed without you either." He swallowed hard. "But Gordon's dead. It's been eight years."

As he spoke the words, the old familiar pain rippled through him. It was less searing than in the past, yet still strong enough to make him pause to regroup his defenses. He inhaled sharply and squared his shoulders. "And you're young and beautiful and very much alive, Jackie. It's time to get on with your life. After all, it's been eight years," he repeated.

Eight years since the untimely death of his twin brother. Nearly nine since the terrible diagnosis of the inoperable brain tumor that had ultimately claimed Gordon McCall's life, leaving his twenty-four-year-old wife a widow, his newborn daughter fatherless, and his twin brother desolate and bereft.

"Eight years," Jackie echoed softly. She moved out of Gray's arms and carried the dinner plates to the table. "Gray, I don't want you to take this the wrong way, but it's time for you to get on with your life too."

"Oh, I have, I have," he assured her. "This year is really looking great. The soccer team is good enough to go all the way to the state finals if we keep our concentration and don't get sidelined by injuries. And I have some really promising students in my Advanced Placement biology class, the kind of kids who come along maybe once a decade. Things are looking terrific, Jackie."

"Terrific," she repeated, arching her brows. "But what I meant was that it's time for you to start looking seriously for someone to—"

"Don't say it!" He held up his hand, as if to playfully ward off her next words. "I get enough of that 'When are you going to find yourself a nice girl and settle down?' stuff from Aunt Kay. So I'll tell you what I always tell her. I'm not interested in settling down. I was married once, and believe me, it's not something I'm in a hurry to repeat."

"You were married to a viper," Jackie said, her eyes flashing with emotion. "That doesn't count. Lily Holden was the most selfish, cold-blooded, completely heartless woman I've ever had the misfortune to know."

"Yeah, and I had the astonishingly poor judgment to marry her," he said dryly. "Not exactly a winning endorsement of my ability to choose a mate, hmm?

Divorce was the best thing that happened in our marriage. Do you blame me for not being eager to repeat the experience?"

"I blame Lily for hurting you when you were already suffering unbearably! For her to begrudge you the time you spent with your dying brother, to walk out on you during the worst time of your life . . ." Jackie choked back a furious sob. "Even eight years later it still gets to me, Gray. She really worked you over, and you've never been the same since. I'd like to kill her for what she's done to you."

"I'm long past being hurt by the specter of Lily, Jackie. She's not the reason why I've become a confirmed bachelor." He actually smiled. "The truth is, I like my life just the way it is. I have a job that I love, and I can devote the necessary hours to the kids in my classes and the soccer team without feeling guilty about neglecting a wife. And I do have a family—you and Mandy and dear old Aunt Kay, who I fervently hope will remain busy with her craft fairs, bridge tournaments, and group trips in far-away Arizona."

His lighthearted humor did not assuage Jackie's intensity. "Gray, I want you to know that Mandy and I will always be your family," she said. "And whatever children Paul and I might have are your family too. I'll never forget what you've done for Mandy and me. How you've been there for us, through Gordon's illness and all the years since his death."

"Now, don't go getting weepy on me," Gray said huskily. "We're family, and nothing will change that."

It was a compassionate lie. His sister-in-law's new marriage would definitely change things, and they both knew it. But Jackie was in love with Paul Whittier, the first man she'd dated since Gordon's death, and happily, Paul returned her feelings.

Gray knew he was glad for them, knew he'd spoken the truth when he said Jackie deserved every happiness. Yet he also knew it would take some time for his painful sense of loss to lessen. He managed to smile at Jackie, then walked to the kitchen door to call Mandy to dinner.

Her dark brown pigtails swinging, the little girl bounded into the kitchen a moment later. She threw her arms around him and gave him a boisterous hug.

"Is Paul coming over tonight?" she asked as she sat down at the table.

Jackie glanced at Gray. "Yes, he is," she said.

"Good!" Mandy said. "I want to show him my spelling paper. I got a one-hundred A. Paul helped me study for the test. He's a real good helper."

"That's terrific, Mandy," Gray said, but inside he felt slightly hollow. He'd been helping Mandy with her spelling since the first grade, but it seemed he'd been supplanted. Then again, his efforts at helping her to study had generally ended with Mandy cajoling him into playing Candyland or Chutes and Ladders instead. She'd never brought home an A on a spelling test before, although she was certainly capable of it.

"As a spelling coach, it seems that Paul has the right stuff," he said, smiling at the child. He cleared his throat. "I bet he has the right stuff as a dad too."

Jackie reached over and laid her hand on his. "Mandy," she said, "I have some very happy news for you. . . ."

The image of the three of them—Mandy, Jackie, and Paul—seated in front of the TV in Jackie's living room, the quintessential picture of family togetherness, stayed with Gray for a long time after he left them there. With that image came a terrible loneliness, so piercing he felt an actual physical ache.

Time was passing, things were changing. The life he'd built around Jackie and Mandy was finally coming to an end. For one gripping moment he visualized the future—himself growing older, living alone, more and more on the periphery of Jackie's and Mandy's lives as they moved on, leaving him behind. Never had Gordon seemed so far away, a shadowy memory from a fast-fading past.

Being Gray, he did not allow himself more than that one dark moment of pain. Quickly he changed into his running clothes and drove to the track, the car radio playing so loudly, it would've been impossible to think, even if he'd wanted to.

He'd run around the track twice when it occurred to him that he was bored, not with running but with the track itself. The thought of a third time around that same ring was intolerable. He wanted the exercise, he needed the physical exertion, but not there.

A thought struck him. Why not run through the surrounding neighborhood? *That* was what he needed, a change of scene. He veered off the track and jogged along the tree-lined sidewalk. Yes, he had definitely made the right decision, he thought as he felt his gloom lifting. It was replaced by a growing sense of anticipation, though of what he wasn't sure.

He ran three blocks, then four.

"Hey, Coach McCall!"

Gray looked up to see Aaron and Andrew Emory walking toward him, the two of them holding onto a leash attached to the collar of an enormous Great Dane.

He was on the street where the Emorys lived! Gray tried to convince himself that he was surprised, that he'd been unaware of the direction he'd been heading. It didn't work. He knew he'd had growing anticipation at the thought of seeing Elissa again.

He stopped in front of the boys and the huge dog. "Is that a pony or a dog?" he asked jokingly. "And more importantly, is he tame or a man-eater?"

"Oh, he's real friendly," Aaron said, patting the dog's immense head. "His name is Jaws."

"Jaws," Gray repeated dryly. "Sounds like a regular lapdog."

"Go ahead and pet him, Coach," Andrew said. "He won't bite."

Gray arched his brows. "Famous last words. But, hey, I hear the medical center in Columbus is doing great work in reattaching severed limbs, so I'll take a chance." He patted the dog's head. Jaws promptly sat down and actually seemed to grin with delight.

"Told you he was friendly," Aaron said. "He likes you, Coach."

"Andrew, Aaron!" The door to the house they were standing in front of had opened, and a little boy about five or six years old came running out. "Guess what happened?" the child called excitedly. "My gerbil had seven babies! Wanna come in and see them? They're in the cage and they're real, real little."

"That's Jared Berman," Andrew explained to Gray. "I baby-sit for him sometimes. Lissa says that me and Aaron are his idols."

"We are," Aaron said. "I guess we'd better go see his gerbils, Andrew."

Jared ran down to join them. "C'mon, you have to see them!" he cried, jumping up and down with excitement.

Andrew and Aaron exchanged rather paternal, amused glances. "Okay, Jared, we'll come see them," Andrew said. He handed the dog's leash to Gray. "Coach McCall, will you walk Jaws down to our yard? Elissa is out front watering the flowers. You can give him to her."

The leash was thrust into his hand before Gray had a chance to refuse. He watched the three boys run into Jared's house, then looked down at the big dog, who was sitting contentedly at his feet. "Let's go, boy," he said, and Jaws obligingly rose and started to trot down the street toward his home.

Elissa was indeed in the front yard, holding a

green garden hose and watering a scraggly patch of geraniums planted under a tall, wide-branched oak tree.

"That's a terrible place for geraniums," the biologist in him couldn't resist saying. "Not enough sun."

If Elissa was surprised to see him, and in possession of Jaws, he saw no hint of it. "Maybe that's why they're not doing too well. I thought it was because I usually forget to water them."

"This time of day, shortly before dark, isn't a good time to water outdoor plants. When it cools off at night, the moisture can cause fungus that—"

"That's enough!" she exclaimed. "I feel as if I'm back in heinous biology lab. Next you'll pull some nauseating, dead creature out of a vat of formaldehyde and expect me to cut it open."

"The term is dissect," he said. Almost compulsively, his gaze swept over her, taking in her peach-colored cotton sundress. The shirred bodice clung to her breasts, molding their contours, and the short, swingy skirt skimmed her knees. She was tanned and young and lovely . . . and they were discussing dissection, formaldehyde, and fungus!

He smiled wryly. He could almost hear Gordon's voice, razzing him: *You need to brush up on your social skills, brother. You've been around schoolkids for way too long.*

Jaws tugged at the leash, trying to break free to go to Elissa. "How did you happen to end up with Jaws?" she asked curiously.

"Courtesy of your little brothers." He released Jaws, who gave a joyous bark and trotted over to Elissa. "They asked me to bring him home while they paid a visit to some newborn gerbils."

She nodded. "Jared's, I presume." She laid down the hose and picked up Jaws's leash, then gave him a curious glance. "So you came over here just to bring Jaws back?"

He shrugged, uncomfortably aware that the truth was more complex—and revealing—than that.

She seemed to accept the shrug as his answer, and looked at the dog. Jaws interpreted her look as encouragement of some sort, for he barked again and stood up on his two hind legs, placing his front paws on her shoulders.

Gray laughed. "You two look like you're dancing together."

"We are. Jaws loves to dance." She put her hands on the dog's body and took a few steps. The dog moved with her. "In fact, he's one of my better partners. He's never yet mashed my foot with his."

The pair box-stepped closer to Gray. Jaws's tongue hung out of his mouth and he drooled blissfully. "Want to dance with him?" Elissa asked, a challenging grin tilting the corners of her mouth. Her eyes were shining as bright as diamonds.

Gray stared at her, transfixed. She moved even closer, all set to transfer Jaws over to him. "No thanks," he said quickly. "Nothing personal, Jaws, but I don't dance with other guys." His eyes met Elissa's. "I'll dance with you, though."

His provocative comment seemed to hang in the air between them. Gray visualized taking her into his arms; Elissa imagined herself being there. Their gazes held for just a moment longer than they should have, crossing an intangible line into acute sensual awareness. Gray felt his heart rate accelerate. Elissa's breathing quickened.

And then swiftly, silently, both pulled back. It was much safer to pretend he'd been joking.

"Nothing personal," she said, looking away from him, "but I promised all my dances to Jaws tonight."

"You're sticking with the guy you came with. Very commendable." Gray cleared his throat and took a deep breath, willing away the telltale beginnings of his sharp, sudden arousal.

An awkward tension threatened, and Jaws—

perhaps sensing something—suddenly dropped down to all fours and began to prance clownishly around the yard. Relieved at the distraction, Elissa and Gray laughed. "You've made him a very happy dog," Gray said.

At that moment Seth's dark blue Plymouth Laser screeched to a halt in front of the house. The boy climbed out of the car and came bounding over to them.

"Hey, Coach!" he greeted Gray enthusiastically. "You here to see me?" He didn't wait for an answer, assuming the affirmative. "The team's a little worried about the Northgate game tomorrow. Their midfielders are all seniors who've been playing varsity since their freshman year. They blew away the Raccoon Township team last week and—"

"What did I tell you guys at practice this afternoon, about the dangers of getting psyched out by another team's reputation?" Gray interrupted calmly. "If that happens, you can lose the game before you ever play it. We're well prepared for Northgate."

"And while we're on the subject of being well prepared," Elissa asked, "have you studied for tomorrow's French test, Seth?" Seth could easily talk soccer all night. French, on the other hand, was not a subject he pursued with much diligence.

"The French teacher loves me. She'll never flunk me," Seth said confidently.

He'd just answered her question. "Go inside, get out your French book, and start studying," Elissa ordered.

"I did study!" Seth said. "I was over at Vicky Drayton's tonight and we were studying French. Honest!" he added as his sister raised her brows skeptically.

"Vicky Drayton?" Gray was surprised. "Is she your new girlfriend?" As coach/father figure/mentor, he tried to take an interest in his players' personal lives, but sometimes high school romances moved too fast for him to keep up with them.

"Oh, I'm still going with Brenda Cooper," Seth said. "Vicky's just a friend. Actually, she spent most of the evening talking about you, Coach." He gave Gray a man-to-man wink. "Vicky's crazy about you. I mean, she's got a *major* crush on you."

Gray thought of giggly, giddy red-haired Vicky Drayton, one of his biology students. She had a crush on him? He nearly groaned aloud. "No, I didn't know," he said. "But it does explain a few things."

"Like why she goes nuts every time she's near you? Like how she follows you around, doing anything to get your attention?" Seth chortled. "Hey, Coach, maybe you should go for it with Vicky. After all, her dad is CEO of the McKnight hotel chain. He's the richest guy in Riverview. You could marry Vicky, retire from teaching, and let her dad set you up in a fancy executive job in Columbus. What do you think? Way cool, huh?"

Gray was too appalled to reply.

"*I* think," Elissa said, "that you and Vicky should have spent more time studying French instead of concocting a plot that sounds as if it came straight from *The Young and the Restless.* Now, hit the books, Seth. *Bonsoir* and *bon chance.*"

Gray was inordinately relieved that Elissa had come to his rescue. "Seth, there's a word for men who lust after little girls, and it isn't *teacher*," he said.

"Vicky's not a little girl," Seth said. "She's really pretty and she has a real hot body. She—"

"—is a child," Gray said firmly. "Look, Seth, I know you students, particularly the seniors, believe your-selves to be quite mature, but teachers see kids as just what they are. Kids." He turned to Elissa. "Isn't that right?"

"Don't expect *her* to agree with you," Seth said before Elissa could speak. Having been reduced to

kid status, he was ready for a little revenge. "Back
when Lissy was in high school, she had a crush on
you that dusted Vicky's current crush." He dramatically hit his forehead with his hand. "I was only in
fourth grade back then, but I can still remember how
she talked and talked and *talked* about you. Like all
the time!"

"Seth," Elissa said sweetly, "I'm going to kill you."

Gray grinned at her. "Is it true?"

"That I'm going to kill my horrible little brother?
Oh, absolutely. You'll have to find another starter for
the team, Coach."

"Not that." Gray laughed. "Did you really have a
crush on me, Elissa?"

"She sure did!" Seth crowed gleefully. "Jeez, Coach
McCall, how could you not have noticed? I mean, it
was eight years ago and I was just a little kid, but
even I knew she was madly in love with you!"

"Eight years ago," Gray repeated thoughtfully.
Eight years ago he'd been grappling with the
breakup of his marriage and the death of his brother.
"I wasn't very aware of what was going on around me
back then," he confessed. "I'm afraid you would've
had to run me down with an eighteen-wheeler to
make me take notice."

"Good thing Elissa didn't know that or she probably would've tried it," Seth said, and laughed uproar-
iously at his own wit.

Gray looked at Elissa. She'd folded her arms in
front of her and was trying to look cool and calm.
Somehow he knew she was anything but. It pleased
him greatly. "So you had a crush on me?"

"No." She sighed. "Oh, all right, I admit it. I did.
But that was a very long time ago. I'm all grown up
and I'm over it now."

"Are you?" The huskiness in his voice surprised
Gray. What surprised him even more was his eagerness to pursue this topic, which was nothing but

awkward for both himself and Elissa. Strangely, he didn't feel awkward. He felt intrigued and excited.

"Oh, yes, I've made a complete recovery," Elissa said. She was mortified by her brother's bald admission, yet bemused by the fact that she'd been so blatantly infatuated with Gray and he had never even guessed. And if that were true, she mused, then why had he run out on her the night before? Not, obviously, because he believed her infatuation was about to rear its ugly head again. It was as puzzling as his showing up there that night. "Silly little-girl crushes," she went on, "are notoriously temporary. A fact for which we all can be grateful."

She forced herself to meet his eyes, then wished she hadn't. The way Gray was looking at her made her feel breathless and set her every nerve ending tingling. Everything around them seemed to be fading from view, leaving just the two of them in an ever-deepening aura of intimacy.

Nonplussed, Elissa quickly turned away from him. Was she falling into that old trap of conjuring up romantic moments that she experienced alone, moments that Gray McCall was totally unaware of? Bad enough to do it at seventeen, but at twenty-five such behavior was inexcusable!

"Hey, Lissy, are you trying to drown those poor flowers, or what?" Seth's voice broke into her thoughts, and she saw him lift the hose from the ground. It was still spraying water, flooding the hapless geraniums.

Gray, too, was startled out of a sensual haze by Seth. He was astonished at how vehemently he wished his star soccer player would disappear, leaving him alone with Elissa.

It was Elissa who disappeared, though, running to the side of the house to turn off the spigot. Jaws followed her, and neither returned. A few minutes later she reappeared on the front porch to call Seth inside.

"Good night, Coach McCall," she added, her voice cool and clear.

Gray watched her step back inside, watched the door close behind her. It took him a few moments to remember that he was supposed to be taking a run through the neighborhood, not standing dumb-struck in front of the Emory house.

He set off at breakneck speed and kept up the pace until he thought his lungs would burst. Even then he kept on running.

Three

Late that night as he lay in bed Gray thrashed the covers about, tossing and turning and wondering why his extra-long run a few hours earlier and the soothing shower hadn't worked its usual magic, sending his fatigued body into a deep, dreamless sleep.

He hated to lie awake and alone, for inevitably his mind conjured up the images he deliberately blocked out during the busy daytime hours. There were his parents, laughing and saying good-bye as they left for the airport, the last time he'd seen them. And his brother, Gordon, getting progressively weaker and sicker, until he finally lapsed into the coma from which he would never emerge. And there was his ex-wife Lily, so heartbreakingly beautiful as she told him that she wanted a divorce, that he was a failure and a disappointment, not at all the man she thought she'd married.

Gray punched the pillow and forced himself to think about the soccer team's game against North-gate High. He mapped out strategy, using each player's strengths against what he knew of the op-posing team. He went through the entire process again and again, even devising alternative plans using the third-string players. Finally, finally, his eyes drifted shut and he fell asleep. . . .

He could smell her scent, feminine and enticing and arousing, as he pressed his lips to her neck. The feel of her soft skin was intoxicating, and he nibbled and tasted as she sighed his name. He kissed his way along her delicate jawline to her mouth, her beautiful mouth, that was soft and sensual and irresistible.

He didn't have to hold back. She wanted him to kiss her, deep and hard, exactly the way he wanted to kiss her. Her lips parted, and his tongue penetrated deep inside her mouth. She met his tongue with her own, and they engaged in a passionate duel that left them both breathless. His hands drifted over her body. He was delighted but not surprised that she was naked, and he savored the warm, silken smoothness of her skin.

Her breasts were full and soft. As he cupped them with his hands, her sighs of pleasure told him that she loved what he was doing as much as he loved doing it. It was dark and he couldn't see her nipples, but his fingers glided unerringly over them, and he smiled when he heard her breathy little whimper.

He felt the tips grow hard and taut and he continued his erotic play. She loved it; the way she moaned his name assured him of that. He took his time with her, touching and relishing the warm, pliant softness before his mouth replaced his hands on her breasts. His tongue circled and stroked until she was writhing beneath him, crying his name.

He slipped his thigh between her long legs, and she tightened around him as she sinuously rubbed his calf with her foot. Her hands caressed him everywhere. She had no shyness, no inhibitions. She knew exactly where and how to touch him to lift him to a fever-pitch of arousal.

She was whispering his name, pleading with him to take her, by the time his hands moved to caress her satiny inner thighs. He felt her hand close greedily around him. She was becoming aggressive, demanding that he enter her now, but he continued his leisurely exploration of her body. He was in no hurry, he was enjoying every moment of their fore-play too much to rush things. Finally his fingers slipped between her thighs to the feathery softness there, and he knew exactly how very, very ready she was for him.

Murmuring intimate, sexy promises, he moved on top of her. It was time to end the sensual torment, wonderful though it was, and satisfy them both. As he positioned himself above her, feeling her body yield to him, he glanced down at her face. Pale blue eyes, glazed with passion stared into his. She was smiling as she caressed his cheek, whispered his name.

"Elissa!" Gray gasped her name, and woke up.

He looked wildly around his bedroom. It was dark and quiet and his bed was empty. He was alone and he'd been dreaming. About making love to Elissa Emory.

He was sweating, panting, his body aroused and throbbing and unsatisfied. He threw off the covers and stalked into the bathroom. Never had he had a dream so profoundly real, never had he been so affected by a dream. Hell, he was still affected! He couldn't stop thinking about her, how passionate and desirable she'd been in the dream, how much he had wanted her. How much he still wanted her.

Cursing, he turned on the shower. The water was cold and he did not adjust it, even as he yelped aloud when it splashed over his overheated body.

It was a dream, just a dream, he told himself as he shivered under the icy spray. That didn't mean he wanted her. He couldn't want her. He refused to want her. She'd been one of his students, for Pete's sake! *And she had been madly in love with him.* The thought leaped unbidden to his mind, and Gray blanched. Had that knowledge inspired his dream? He'd meant what he had said to Seth. Little girls held no appeal for him, and he regarded all his students as youngsters. When Elissa had been seventeen and infatuated with him, he'd never noticed. Even if he had, it wouldn't have mattered. She'd been a child.

But she wasn't now. The words seemed to echo in the night, as if he'd spoken them aloud. His still-hot body burned at the implication, until his stern, disciplined mind once again wrested control of his raging libido.

Though Elissa Emory was no longer a schoolgirl, she was still too young for him. After all, she was twenty-five to his thirty-four. And when those numbers didn't seem at all outrageous and unacceptable, he reminded himself that when she was in kindergarten playing with dolls and taking naps, he'd been fourteen years old, wearing braces and lusting after Mary Alice Beamon.

And when *that* seemed irrelevent, too, all his defenses leaped into the fray. Ages aside, the truth was that Elissa Emory was all wrong for him. She was way too emotional. A woman like her would demand that the man she was sleeping with be . . . well, *involved* with her, and not just physically. Totally.

He wanted no part of an emotionally demanding, complex involvement with a woman. He was too old for that, too weary, too hardened, and too cynical. He'd already gone the in-love-forever route, and the thought of enduring another soul-destroying relationship made his blood run cold.

Or maybe it was the frigid water pulsing down on him that was chilling his blood. It was certainly freezing his skin; he felt as if he were turning blue. He'd better end this arcticlike shower before hypothermia set in.

Turning off the taps, Gray stepped out of the shower and swiftly wrapped himself in his thick terry toweling robe. Though he felt as if he'd been flash-frozen, his sanity had been restored. There would be no more desperate thoughts and urgent yearnings for Elissa Emory that night. Or ever again, he promised fiercely, heading back into his bedroom.

"This is the volleyball team?" Elissa looked at the eight girls standing before her in the gym. They stared silently back at her.

Upon hiring her as Riverview's art teacher, Ursula Warburton, the school's imposing, imperious principal, had requested that Elissa take on two additional duties: adviser to the cheerleaders and coach of the fledgling girls' volleyball team. As a former cheerleader, Elissa had accepted the cheerleader-adviser role without qualms. Coaching volleyball was a different story.

She'd initially refused on the grounds of knowing nothing about the sport, except the little she remembered from high school gym classes. The ever-persistent Miss Warburton had supplied her with a coach's manual and a wrenching tale of the regular coach's unfortunate hospitalization and of the disappointment of all the eager young players who would be deprived of participating in the sport dearest to their hearts if no one replaced their coach. Nobody else on the faculty had volunteered for the position. If Elissa didn't take it, there would be no girls' volleyball team.

Elissa surrendered to the inevitable. She studied the manual every night before going to bed, and she'd announced this practice, her first with the team, three days earlier. A reminder had been repeated over the school's public-address system during the following morning and afternoon announcements. All those enthusiastic, eager players that Miss Warburton had assured her were on the volleyball team should have known about the practice and shown up for it.

So where were they? At least six players were required for a volleyball team. Five potential players stood before her. The other three girls . . .

"You can't be the entire team," she said, her tone laced with a mixture of pleading and incredulity.

She knew those other three girls—Rachel, Shannon, and Donna—from her art classes, and they were not players of any sport. These girls, in their expensive coordinated outfits, with their elaborate hairstyles and cover-girl makeup, were princesses. Elissa knew the type well. This particular breed of girl avoided anything that might cause sweating. They viewed even cheerleaders as steroid-swigging jocks. Female athletes were beyond their imagination.

"We're the volleyball team," said one of the Kovach twins, though Elissa had no idea which one she was. "Believe it or not."

"I prefer *not*," said Shannon, a tall platinum blonde who looked as if she were a high-fashion model on her way to a layout shoot.

"With that kind of team spirit, how can we possibly win even a single game?" asked Laretha Warren, one of the stars of the girls' track team. She was competitive and fast and would be a serious player, Elissa knew. "I wanted an indoor fall sport, but I never dreamed *they* would sign up for volleyball. Why did you?"

"We needed a sport for our college résumés," explained Donna, a honey-blonde who was shorter than Shannon, but equally glamorous. "So we signed up for volleyball, never dreaming we might actually have to play."

"We had two earlier practices this summer with Coach Marsh," said a striking redhead, whom Elissa knew was Vicky Drayton, "but they managed not to play at either. All three of them had medical excuses from their doctors."

"Undoubtedly forged," Laretha said.

"When Coach Marsh went into the hospital," Shannon said to Elissa, "we thought we were finished with this volleyball nonsense, until we heard that awful announcement over the PA. Miss Emory, I'm an artist, as you well know from my creativity in art class. Surely, you wouldn't make *me* play!"

"Those three know nothing about volleyball," said Adrienne Simms. She was on two swimming teams, had set a county diving record, and obviously had no use at all for unathletic princess types. "They probably think the terms *set, volley, spike,* and *serve* have to do with hair and nail care."

Elissa considered the situation. Her team was in dire straights. They had no depth at all; there was no one to replace the five girls who knew what they were doing and wanted to play. Those five would have to be in the game every minute, with no time out for rest or injury. And the sixth player would have to be either Rachel, Shannon, or Donna, a truly daunting thought.

She watched the girls glaring at each other, five versus three, each side equally disdainful of the other. There was certainly no team spirit here, and there seemed to be no solution. For a moment she actually envied Coach Marsh's timely hospital stay, but she knew she had to take charge.

"Everyone, please sit down," she said, and waited until the girls were sitting on the bleachers.

"We need all eight of you," she went on, "six to play and two as back up. We're a team and we have a schedule of games with other schools already set. We're going to play them, not forfeit." Not exactly Knute Rockne, she acknowledged, but at least everyone was listening. "So since we're all here, let's get the net set up and practice."

Adrienne, Laretha, Vicky, the Kovach twin, and the fifth girl, Bethany Becker, who was short, thin, and looked about twelve years old, all helped Elissa assemble the net. The other three girls watched from the bleachers.

"We'll line up, four on each side," Elissa directed. "Who wants to serve first? Shannon, how about you?"

Shannon recoiled in horror. "Why me?"

"Come on, it's not going to be that bad." Elissa gave her an encouraging smile.

"Well, you'll have to show me how, because I don't know what to do."

To get things going, Elissa stood on one side and served the ball. Unfortunately she was as bad at serving now as she had been in high school. She hit the ball with the soft, sensitive inside of her wrist, and pain radiated the whole way up her arm. She winced, certain she was going to have a bruise.

"Uh, Miss Emory, it's easier and less painful if you do it this way," Laretha said helpfully, and demonstrated the correct way to serve. The ball sailed over the net, and Adrienne nearly knocked Donna over as she jumped forward to return it.

Donna crashed into the Kovach twin, grabbed onto her for balance, then let go, emitting a piercing scream. "Oh no! I broke a nail!"

Rachel and Shannon rushed over to console her, while Adrienne and Laretha exchanged looks of exasperation.

"You can take care of your nail later," Elissa said. "Vicky, you serve this time."

As Vicky picked up the ball, the doors to the gym burst open. A group of boys thundered in, laughing and shouting, then stopped dead at the sight of the girls.

"It's the soccer team!" Adrienne exclaimed.

"*He* must be with them!" Vicky said hoarsely, dropping the ball.

As if on cue, Gray walked into the gym. Elissa heard Vicky gasp. She herself felt like groaning. She hadn't seen Gray for the past four days, not since

Seth had informed him of that long-ago crush she'd had on him. She had an unnerving feeling that the subject was not closed, and she wasn't looking forward to rehashing it with him.

"He's wearing jeans!" Vicky whispered. "Ohh, he looks so hot!"

Elissa closed her eyes in horror. She'd played this scene before, with herself in the infatuated-Vicky role. How she hated reliving it! But almost compulsively her eyes opened and focused on Gray. He *was* wearing jeans, and nobody wore them better. His muscular arms and shoulders were emphasized by his burgundy knit shirt too.

Gray spotted Elissa the moment he walked into the gym. Involuntarily, he balled his hands into fists. The last time he'd seen her had been in that dream that had played like one of those fantasy letters to *Penthouse* come to life. She had been naked and hot and eager, and he'd been actively avoiding her ever since, even to the point of eating his lunch in the biology lab—an unappetizing prospect to be sure. He did it anyway; he was *that* unsettled about seeing her.

Now here she was, and a meeting between them was inevitable. For a long moment, he stood frozen to the spot, uncertain of what to do or say, feeling as gauche and callow as a sweaty-palmed adolescent.

"Coach, what are these girls doing in here?" one of his players asked.

It was just the impetus Gray needed to pull himself together. Ultimately he'd always been able to do what had to be done. He strode toward Elissa, telling himself he had no other recourse. After all, she was the only other adult present. He tried to ignore the accelerated pounding of his pulses, but he couldn't restrain himself from staring at her. She was wearing plaid boxer-style shorts and a bright green T-shirt. Her legs were long and slim, and he remembered how they'd felt against his, how he had stroked her silky skin. . . .

A flash of heat tore through him. *He didn't remember because he'd never touched her legs. He'd only dreamed it!* But the dream had seemed so vivid, so real. Worse, he kept reliving it, during odd times of the day and compulsively at night. A deep flush heated his neck and face. He felt guilty as a prurient schoolboy.

Elissa walked forward to meet him. She was frowning, which rattled him even more. There was no way she could know what he'd been thinking, what he had dreamed, he assured himself. But why was she looking at him that way? So cool and definitely disapproving.

"What are you doing here?" she asked, keeping her eyes focused on some point to his left.

She was irritated by their presence; there could be no doubt of that. Gray found himself fighting a smile. Elissa wore her emotions on her sleeve, and though he claimed displays of emotions made him uncomfortable, it was actually icy withdrawal that disturbed him. His ex-wife had been cold, distant, and aloof; even in good times he'd had difficulty reading her. Elissa was so different. She let everybody know how she felt. And right now she clearly was impatient for an answer to her question.

"I was about to ask you the same thing," he said. "We're here because it started to rain in the middle of soccer practice. It's pouring out there, with thunder and lightning, so we came inside to work out."

"Well, I reserved the gym for volleyball practice this afternoon," she said sternly. "You and your team are on our time, and you'll have to leave."

His eyes widened and he gave a sudden laugh. *"Volleyball practice?"*

"I'm the coach of the team," Elissa said. She took a deep breath and ignored his incredulous yelp of laughter. "And yes, we're practicing. Our first game is early next week." *Heaven help them*, she added silently.

"Wait a minute, I can't take this all in at once." Gray was really laughing now. "Are my eyes playing tricks on me, or do I see Rachel, Shannon, and Donna? This must be the first time any of them has ever set foot in the Riverview gym. As for actually *playing* a game, I've never seen them move faster than a slow stroll."

"Laretha, Adrienne, and the Kovach twin are all fine athletes," she said, loyally defending her team. "And the other girls have . . . um, spirit." She glared at him. "Stop laughing!"

"I'm sorry." He held up his hand, as if to ward off the laughter claiming him. It didn't work. He tried to collect himself and start over. "As a coach, I know how important . . . er, spirit is, but to actually win a game, a team needs much more. Talent, skill, strength, size, depth."

"We have all that," Elissa said crossly. "We just need to develop it. And as the coach, it's my job to help them do it." She lifted her head and squared her shoulders in newfound determination.

Gray grinned. "If you get Donna Lydon to even *touch* a ball, you've got my vote for coach of the year."

Elissa looked at him, Riverview's winningest coach, with a soccer team already rated number one in the state of Ohio and currently ranked nationally in *USA Today*'s High School Soccer Poll. How damnably smug of him to make coach-of-the-year jokes to her! "You don't think we can win a single game, do you?"

He covered his smile with his hand. "Hmm, how can I put this tactfully?"

"Forget tact, just answer the question."

"Okay. No. I don't think you have a prayer of winning a single game with that crew."

Until that moment she hadn't, either, but something in his dark, dancing eyes, something in his sexy smile, made her want to argue with him, to take the opposite side and bait him until . . . Elissa gulped. Until what? All her instincts warned her that she was treading on dangerous ground here.

Furthermore, his smile was not sexy, she reprimanded herself. It was insufferably arrogant, and this was not about sex. Involuntarily her gaze flicked over him, over his broad shoulders and chest and the splendidly masculine fit of his jeans.

She jerked her head, forcing herself to look away, momentarily feeling as giddy and unstrung as poor, lovesick Vicky Drayton, who came bouncing over at that very moment.

"Coach McCall, your team stole our ball!" Vicky exclaimed, giggling. "Does that mean we should play volleyball with this?" She brandished a soccer ball. "Want to serve it while they're kicking around our ball?" She moved closer to him, holding out the ball.

"They're kicking the volleyball?" Gray took the soccer ball absently, his attention focused on the boys, who most definitely were kicking the volleyball around the gym, sending it smashing into walls and whooping with laughter. The ball was soft and not made for such abuse. "Hey!" he hollered. "Cut it out!"

He strode toward the boys, leaving a sighing Vicky behind. "Give the girls their ball back."

"Okay. Here's your ball, *girls*!" Seth said, and sent the deflated ball dribbling toward them.

Adrienne picked it up. It was mushy and shapeless, like a grapefruit rind whose insides had been sucked out. "Here, Miss Emory," she said, carrying it to Elissa. "They killed it. I guess practice is over."

Elissa examined the ball. It was well and truly dead. They couldn't use it for practice, and trekking the whole way down to the supply room to get another one seemed a futile effort. At least three of her players would be long gone before the new ball could be fetched. Better to start anew on another day.

"Let's call it a day," she said. "We'll—"

"Excuse me, Miss Emory," Gray interrupted her. "The boys would like to apologize to you and your team." He had joined them, the boys crowded behind him. They chorused a sheepish apology, then Gray launched into a stern lecture on respecting school property and the rights of others.

Elissa listened, astonished that he was taking the incident so seriously. The girls stood rooted to the spot, transfixed.

"It's like we really are a team who deserves respect," Bethany Becker whispered in awe.

"Of course we are," Elissa assured her.

When Gray's lecture was over, the boys dropped to the floor to do the twenty push-ups the coach demanded as atonement for their misdeed. The girls drifted off to gather their things to go home. Elissa stood, holding the unfortunate ball, watching the boys. She was fully aware that Seth, a leader on the team, had been ringleader in the afternoon's antics, and she was grateful that Gray had handled the discipline as the coach.

"Elissa, I really am sorry about what happened." Gray joined her, glancing ruefully at the ball.

"The girls appreciated the fact that you took it seriously. I do, too, although I'm amazed that you did. I know our team is a joke to you." She flashed a sudden smile, remembering the comical look on his face when he'd learned who was on the volleyball team—and who was coaching it. "But I guess we're a joke with rights, hmm? Like even a joke deserves respect."

His lips quirked. "You're not a joke."

"No?" She tilted her head, still smiling. "A hopeless case, then? A lost cause?"

"You tell me." Their eyes met, and a frisson of sensual electricity surged between them, almost tangible in its intensity. Both felt it, though neither dared to acknowledge it. Still, neither moved. Neither looked away.

And then the intimate interlude was shattered.

"Miss Emory," Laretha called, her exasperated tone piercing the private cocoon that had enveloped Gray and Elissa. "Will you tell these lamebrains that there is more than one volleyball, that practice is not canceled forever, and that the team isn't being disbanded?"

Elissa and Gray turned to see Donna, Shannon, and Rachel glaring at Laretha, who was regarding the three of them with unconcealed scorn.

Gray grinned. Suddenly he felt lighthearted, inexplicably eager and exuberant. "I'm afraid it's true, ladies," he said. "There are lots of volleyballs around, and practice will resume—" He glanced at Elissa. "When will practice resume, Coach?"

"The day after tomorrow," she replied. "Right after school. We'll meet here in the gym."

"Great! See you then, Miss Emory," Laretha said and dashed off.

Rachel, Shannon, and Donna left, shaking their heads in despair.

Gray watched them go, then turned back to Elissa. He couldn't seem to keep from smiling.

She noticed. "You're enjoying this, aren't you? There's some perverse streak in you that takes delight in anticipating an athletic catastrophe, providing that you're not coaching it."

"Hey, no, really, I admire your courage. It takes real guts to coach a team as . . . er, diverse as yours."

"Now try saying that with a straight face," she challenged him. "Aha! You can't."

She was right, he couldn't. The thought of her hapless volleyball team made him smile; the idea of them playing competitively cracked him up. "I'll be at your first game," he promised. "In fact I intend to catch every home game that I can. I'll be sure to inform the yearbook editors and the *Riverview Gazette*'s sports press, too, because they'll want a photographic record of your season. I mean, you've got the classic Cinderella team here, complete with three authentic princesses and—"

"Oh, please do come to the games," she cut in. "I'm going to *love* watching the expression on your face when we win." Her eyes were gleaming, and he knew she was enjoying this as much as he was. "And we will, you know. We'll win at least one game this season, and we'll improve our record next season, and keep on improving every year until we're nationally ranked, just like your soccer team."

"Mm-hmm. And I bet you still believe in the Easter bunny and the Tooth Fairy too."

"And I bet you that we are going to win one, maybe even two games, this season."

He arched his brows. "I think you're starting to suffer from delusions of grandeur. If I take this bet, what are the stakes?"

She didn't hesitate. "I have to chaperone the fall dance that the cheerleaders are sponsoring at the end of October. If the team wins, you have to take my place and be the chaperone that night. Our schedule of games will be over by then, so we'll know who wins—or loses—the bet."

"If I lose—that is, if your team wins one game—I have to chaperone a high school dance? Whew! What a fate. Good thing I don't stand a chance of losing. I loathe high school dances, and I loathe chaperoning them even more."

"Same here. And now that I have a chance of getting out of it, I'll have a real incentive to make the team win." She tossed him a teasing, provocative smile. "Shine your dancing shoes, Gray, because you're going to be at that dance." She started to walk away.

Impulsively he reached out and caught her wrist,

restraining her. "You're pretty sure of yourself, huh? Issuing a promise and a threat all rolled into one."

His fingers tightened, and he felt her soft skin, the delicately shaped bone, and her pulse, which had quickened at his touch. An inexorable urge to pull her closer rushed through him. He was much stronger than she. All he had to do was give a tug and she would come to him.

Instead she winced with pain.

He immediately dropped her wrist. "Did I hurt you?" he asked.

She rubbed her wrist gingerly. "Not you. The volleyball. I hit it so hard with the inside of my wrist, it's already turning black and blue."

He moved closer to look. A fresh bruise was visible on the underside of her wrist. He had the strangest desire to touch his lips to it, to kiss it better. Of course he did no such thing.

He straightened into an almost military posture. "It looks sore," he mumbled. "I'm sorry. I didn't help by manhandling you."

An awkward tension rose between them, and Elissa desperately sought to dispel it. Humor seemed an apt way to restore the easy companionship they'd been enjoying until he'd touched her. "Are you sure you don't want to call off the bet?" she teased. "The stakes are pretty high. Aren't you getting scared?"

"Scared?" He had to laugh at that. "Not hardly, Coach. But it occurs to me that I ought to set some stakes of my own. For example, what if I win? Sure, I won't have to chaperone that dance, but there should be more. Something that you have to do for me. Like . . . oh, I don't know. Washing my car, maybe? Including vaccuming the insides, plus a wax job?"

She made a face. "Couldn't it be some other chore? I know. I could make dinner for you. I'm a great cook. At least my dad and my brothers think so."

He considered it. "So if I win this bet, you'll cook

dinner for me?" In view of his hopeless cooking skills, it seemed too good to pass up. "It can't be spaghetti, though," he added, thinking of his sister-in-law's rather uninspired menu.

"A three-course meal—soup, salad, an entree—not spaghetti. Plus dessert."

"I'm hungry already. You've got a bet."

They shook on it.

"Too bad you're going to lose," she said over her shoulder as she headed for the girls' locker room. "You'll never get that dinner, and I hope you have lots of fun at the fall dance."

"Sorry, honey, you've got it backward," he called after her. "You may as well start planning the menu, because I'm going to win. And I hope *you* have lots of fun at the dance."

Four

"Oh well," Donna Lydon said cheerfully as she, Rachel, and Shannon strolled out of the gym, every hair in place, every polished nail unbroken. "As my daddy always says, you win some and you lose some. You can't let it get to you."

The rest of Riverview's girls' volleyball team watched them leave.

"Well, it sure gets to me! Twenty-one to zero!" Flushed and furious, Adrienne Simms paced back and forth, her hands and jaw clenched. "A complete shutout! I can't believe we didn't even score a single point!"

"It wasn't for lack of trying on your part, Adrienne," Elissa said. "You gave it your all. You put forth one hundred and ten percent effort."

"And for what?" Laretha said. She looked as hot and angry as Adrienne. "I've never played so hard and done so badly before. Did you see the other team laughing at us? *Laughing!* 'cause we're so terrible. I've never been so humiliated in my whole life."

"It was only our first game," Elissa said, trying to sound bolstering and upbeat. "We'll improve. We just have to practice, practice, practice, and not give up."

"Miss Emory," Laretha said, "it doesn't matter how much we practice. We'll still stink because we have three and a half idiots on our team who can't and won't—"

"Am I the half-idiot?" Bethany asked. There was no doubt of the identity of the other three.

"Not you, Bethany," Laretha said, her voice softening. "You really tried hard and you got the ball over the net a few times too. I'm talking about *her*!" She unsubtly pointed her thumb at Vicky. All gazes fell on the red-haired teen who was bouncing up and down, seemingly in constant motion as she chattered with Gray McCall.

Adrienne nodded in agreement. "Vicky played okay in practice, but the minute I saw Coach McCall walk into the gym, I knew we were doomed. She goes completely mental when he's around. Miss Emory, could you tell Coach McCall not to come to our games? Without him around, Vicky might be able to concentrate on playing."

"Here he comes!" Laretha whispered. "Tell him now, Miss Emory."

Gray, dressed in soccer shorts and a black Riverview T-shirt, walked over to them, Vicky skipping and talking animatedly alongside him like a boisterous, yapping puppy. He seemed to regard her as such, smiling indulgently at her.

"I watched about half of the game," he said to the four teammates who stood staring somewhat reproachfully at him. "And I just wanted to tell you that I saw some memorable plays."

"Even *he's* making fun of us now!" Bethany exclaimed, suddenly tearful. She turned and ran from the gym.

Gray looked baffled. "What was that all about? I was about to congratulate you four girls on making a valiant effort despite . . . er, certain adverse factors working against you."

Laretha scowled. "Coach, the team played awful and we all know it." She stomped off.

"Everyone's feeling a bit upset right now," Elissa said quickly. "I'd better go talk to Bethany and Laretha and try to calm them down."

"No, we'll do that, Miss Emory," Adrienne said. "You stay here and . . . uh, talk to Coach McCall. Come on, Vicky, you're going with us." She grabbed Vicky's arm and dragged her off, the Kovach twin following in their wake.

Gray and Elissa faced each other. Amusement glinted in his eyes. "Despite what your team seems to think, I didn't come over here to razz you about your loss. Some of your girls played their hearts out today. But as for the rest . . ."

"Let the razzing begin," Elissa said dryly.

Gray could not hold back a smile. "Lord, Elissa, they were terrible! No, much worse than terrible. They were—"

"I know, I know. So now you're razzing *and* gloating. You should be ashamed of yourself, Coach McCall."

"I probably should. But I keep thinking of my gastronomic payoff at the end of volleyball season. Beef Wellington, veal scaloppini, chicken Kiev. The possibilities are endless."

"As I told the girls, this is only our first game. We're going to get better and we're going to win." She tilted her head and gazed challengingly at him. "So I suggest you begin to listen to heavy-metal and rap tapes to immunize yourself against them, because that's all you'll be hearing for three solid hours at the Fall Dance. Oh, and did I mention they'll be played at full volume? Earplugs might be a wise investment."

"Then you'd better invest in them." He grinned wickedly. "Because you'll be needing them, Coach. There's no way you're not going to be chaperoning that wretched dance—*and* cooking a six-course dinner for me."

"Six? I thought it was three, plus dessert."

"When I saw how hopeless your team is in action, I raised the stakes."

"Six courses." She frowned thoughtfully. "What does that include? It better not be anything too exotic, or my dad and my brothers won't eat. They're basically meat-and-potatoes-type guys. Tuna-noodle casserole is a stretch for them."

"Your dad and your brothers?" echoed Gray. It occurred to him that they had conflicting expectations concerning the payoff. Elissa thought he would be joining the Emory clan for the meal she prepared, but he had been envisioning a completely different scenario, one sans kid brothers and dear old dad. One featuring the two of them alone, at his place.

"They aren't included," he said, and though he'd intended to sound teasing and light, his tone carried an unmistakable intensity.

Elissa's heart skipped a beat. Did that mean Gray wanted to be alone with her? Frustration roiled within her. If that were the case, why didn't he simply ask her out, instead of constantly running hot and then cold with her? She decided it was time to play it like he did. Cool. Confusing. Incomprehensible.

"Well, it doesn't matter anyway, since you're going to lose." She was pleased at the airy nonchalance in her voice and turned to gather up her things. Gray waited, falling in step beside her as she headed out of the gym.

He kept stealing glances at her as they walked through the dim, musty hallway. From this angle he realized how much smaller she was than he. The top of her head came just to his shoulder. His gaze followed the line of her thick ash-blond hair, which swung freely as she moved, parting at times to reveal the slender curve of her neck. Her skin there looked so white and soft, untouched and vulnerable.

Gray caught his breath, feeling as if he'd been

dealt a blow in the gut. The urge to touch her was so strong, he found himself flexing his fingers in preparation. She was so close, and it would be so easy. . . . All he had to do was wrap his hand around her nape and pull her into him. She would lift her head, part her lips, and then . . .

Elissa came to a sudden halt. Aware that he'd been staring hard at her, Gray quickly blinked and looked away. He felt tension heat and stretch within him. Had she seen the fierce, undisguised lust burning in his eyes? He grew angry with himself for responding to her like this, when she had done nothing to evoke such sexual hunger within him. Nothing except be near him, looking sexy and sweet, fueling his fantasies and inspiring flaming needs.

He gritted his teeth. He didn't have time for this nonsense and he refused to give in to it.

Elissa was smiling up at him, though, and he felt the effects of that smile all through his already overheated body. He stifled a moan. How could just one look from her level him so effectively?

"I'm going into the locker room to talk with the girls before they leave," she said.

"Don't just talk at the kids, make them really listen to you. They're in need of an attitude adjustment, and as coach, it's up to you to see that it happens."

"Mmm, sure. And after I adjust everyone's attitude and turn them into a team of compatible, competitive winners, I'll move on to easier things, like solving Russia's economic problems and bringing peace to the Middle East."

She made him smile. She'd always been able to, even during those dark days eight years ago when he'd been in a living hell and she'd been a giddy teenager. *With a major crush on him.* His jaw tightened and he realized that he would not be averse to her having a major crush on him now.

All his self-protective bachelor instincts kicked in

at once. "Look, maybe this bet isn't such a good idea. It's hardly fair to—"

"Chickening out?" she asked. "That means you forfeit, Coach McCall. Consider yourself the official chaperone of the Riverview Fall Dance. I'll see that the cheerleaders are in touch with you about the details." She started to walk away.

"No! Hey, wait a minute."

"Oh, you'll have fun," she called back. "I'm sure Vicky will be thrilled to get you out on the dance floor. It'll be the culmination of a fantasy for her."

The thought of having to dance with his students, especially a smitten one, was too dreadful even to contemplate. "The bet's not off!" he shouted.

Elissa was already opening the door to the locker room, but she paused, letting it slam shut again. "I'll have to think about that."

He strode to her side. "There's nothing to think about it. The bet stands."

"Uh-uh. Since you bowed out, it has to be officially reinstated. And before I agree, I have a few conditions that must be met."

He ran his hand through his hair, simultaneously exasperated and amused. "You're a regular barracuda, Emory," he drawled. "State your conditions."

"Actually there's only one. You can't come to any more of our games. The girls believe that you distract Vicky too much, and after her performance today I'm inclined to agree. In our straits, we need every playable player we have in top form."

He groaned. "Will you quit with this Vicky nonsense? As I told your brother, I have absolutely no interest in any of my students beyond a teacher's normal concern."

"I believe you. But Vicky isn't about to give up, and as long as you're around, her mind won't be on volleyball."

"You're an expert in the field of adolescent crushes, hmm?" Gray asked dryly. "Should I conclude that you're drawing from your own experience?"

"Ohh! That was low, McCall!" She tried to laugh off her embarrassment. It was inevitable that he would make some sort of comment about her erstwhile crush. She'd been expecting it.

And she retaliated immediately. "In fact, that was fiendishly low." Reacting instinctively, she gave him a playful but firm push. Having grown up with four rough and tumble brothers, she'd learned to counter merciless teasing with physical action.

Gray reacted with the quick precision of a natural, experienced athlete. Her push wasn't hard enough to set him off balance, although he did take a step backward to brace himself. At the same time, he caught both her hands before she could pull them away, trapping her.

Compulsively his gaze swept over her, from the tousled hair on her head to the dainty ballet-style slippers on her feet. She was wearing an oversized white shirt, though perhaps it was a dress. It was cinched at the waist with a wide multicolor belt, and below it she wore tight-fitting coral leggings that ended at the ankle. He'd seen some of his students in similar attire, but none of them looked as sexy and stylish as Elissa.

He continued to stare at her as he held her hands, unable to drag his gaze away. His mouth was dry, and he knew he had to say something. He couldn't keep her there, her hands pinned to his chest while he gazed at her in rapt admiration.

"You sure don't look like any coach I've ever seen," he murmured at last. The effect of her nearness was electrifying. A hot shaft of desire bolted through him and he realized he was already fighting for self-restraint.

His proximity was having a similarly wild effect upon Elissa, but she managed to say in a light, albeit shaky, voice, "I hope you don't ascribe to that sexist school of thought that decrees a female coach has to be a troll with thick ankles and a bad haircut."

Tugging on her hands, he pulled her closer. Elissa never thought to protest. Somehow, it was inevitable that this would happen.

"I'm not a sexist," he said, "and believe me, you're no troll." Grinning roguishly, he made an elaborate, overexaggerated inspection of her from head to toe. "Your ankles and your haircut are first-rate too."

Her gaze held his. "Think so?"

"Oh, yeah. In fact, all of you . . ." His voice, deep and raspy, trailed off. Slowly his hand moved to the slender curve of her throat, his fingers spreading to cup the nape of her neck.

Murmuring a soft exclamation, Elissa curled her fingers over his wrist. The action brought her closer to him, so close that her breasts brushed his chest, so close that their thighs touched.

A sweet heat flared within her. She was trembling and breathless as she gazed into his eyes. The corridor began to spin, and everything around seemed to disappear, leaving her and Gray alone in a dizzying sensual whirl. She felt his other hand on her waist, felt his arm go around her and pull her into him. He held her, settling her intimately against his hard frame. She melted into him, accommodating herself to him perfectly.

Gray felt his heart stop, then start to pound wildly, the blood roaring in his ears. This was how it had been in his dream, the way he knew it would be between them in bed, with her giving herself to him, fitting him as if she'd been specially designed for him. Between her parted thighs he felt the softness of her femininity nudging his erection.

Elissa lifted her face to him at the moment he lowered his head to her. Their gazes locked, and a heavy sensual silence engulfed them. Closer, closer, their mouths moved in exquisite anticipation. In another moment their lips would touch—

"Aha! So that's the way it is!"

The hearty, chipper voice seemed to ricochet through the hall like a gunshot. Elissa and Gray simultaneously gasped in shock and jumped away from each other. Both were equally dismayed to see the petite brunette with the short, straight hair standing before them, grinning gleefully. She looked a bit like a manic pixie, Elissa thought, and stifled a moan.

"Connie," she said weakly.

Her voice throbbed, and the sound of it, sexy and throaty, affected Gray viscerally. His whole body was shaking in reaction, shocking proof of how profound his close encounter with Elissa Emory had been. He'd touched her and completely lost his head! The revelation was shattering, the loss of control and composure horrifying to him. They'd been caught in a hot clinch in the halls of Riverview High School! What was happening to him?

He looked down at Elissa and felt a surge of panic mixed with intense resentment. *She* had happened to him! After all these years, just when he'd finally considered himself safe from emotions and entanglements, when he'd finally discovered the right prescription of exercise and hard work to sublimate his sex drive, *she* showed up to drive him into a frenzy of needs he had thought—hoped!—were long dead.

He backed away, his gaze darting frantically from a still-dazed Elissa to a thoroughly amused and curious Connie Ware. "We were . . . um . . ." He cleared his throat and tried again. "This—It isn't what it might've looked like." He wanted to deny the scene as much to himself as to Connie. "Not what it seems."

"'In the real world as in dreams, nothing is quite what it seems,'" Connie quoted.

"No New Age mysticism, please! This is simply a case of . . . It's not as if . . ." He broke off, glumly aware that he was babbling incoherently.

"You don't have to try to explain anything to me," Connie said cheerfully. "Not that you were doing a very good job of it anyway."

Elissa winced. "Connie, what are you doing here?"

"A question I'd better not ask you guys, hmm?" Connie was thoroughly enjoying herself. "Anyway, I'm here for the adult literacy program. I tutor adults in reading once a week from five-thirty to seven."

"Five-thirty?" Gray seized on that the way a drowning man would grasp for a life preserver in a stormy sea. "It's five-thirty already?" He looked at his watch to confirm the hour, as if some appointment really did await him. "Oh, hey, I'm late. Jeez, five-thirty! I—um . . ." He nodded to Connie, but didn't dare glance in Elissa's direction. It was as if she were a powerful witch who had cast a potent spell on him. If he didn't flee now, he would be forever ensnared.

"I'll see you around," he muttered to no one in particular, then took off down the hall without looking back.

"Whew! That was one quick getaway." Connie shook her head. "Sorry, Lissy. I guess I should have tiptoed past or something but—"

"It's okay, Con," Elissa cut in briskly. She was well aware that her friend would have been constitutionally unable to slip discreetly by without comment.

"At least it was me and not ole Warburton!" Connie crowed. "Imagine, two teachers groping each other in the hall being caught by the principal." The image seemed to please her, for she laughed in delight.

Elissa was not similarly delighted. "I'd rather not imagine it." She put her icy hands to her flushed cheeks. "Connie, we've been friends for a long time, haven't we?"

Connie nodded, and Elissa continued, "Will you do me a favor? A big one?"

"Sure, Lissy. Anything."

"Never mention this—this scene with Gray McCall again, okay? I don't want to talk about it or—"

"Not talk about it?" Connie wailed. "But Elissa, considering how crazy you were about Gray as a kid and how you ended up back in Riverview High and now here you are, making out in the hall with him, I'd say it's Destiny! It's Fate, it must be! How can we not talk about something as momentous and wondrous as that?"

"Gray McCall has no intentions of simply bowing to Destiny's wishes," Elissa said. "Fate's either. I—I think he's attracted to me, but he hates that he is. That much he made clear by the speed record he set getting away from here. Not to mention the way he looked at me, as if I'd deliberately stolen his reason and his common sense and *made* him . . ." She paused and swallowed, her voice lowering. ". . . touch me."

"Not to mention that," Connie said, sighing sadly, "the way he took off was kind of, well, unchivalrous."

"There's more to it than that." Elissa wondered why she felt the need to defend Gray. He had attempted to deny that their moment of interrupted passion had meant anything to him, then had hot-footed it away from her. A sudden insight struck her. "He pulls back when we start to get close, as if—"

"Aargh! Not another commitment-phobic man!" Connie screwed up her face in disapproval. "I wasted three years on one of those weasels!"

Elissa frowned. "He's not one of those."

"That's what every commitment-phobic wants you to believe. That with you, this time, it'll be different. Ha!"

"Well, what about Destiny and Fate?" Elissa couldn't resist asking. "Wasn't that your first diagnosis?"

"I don't pretend to know *all* the answers, Elissa."

"Just remember your promise," Elissa reminded her. She pushed open the locker-room door and headed inside.

"I didn't see a thing," Connie called after her. "So there's nothing to talk about, is there?"

"Nothing," Elissa repeated, her head spinning in a whirl of confusion and anger so thoroughly enjoined, she couldn't begin to separate them. "Nothing at all."

Five

At the soccer game several days later Riverview High took an immediate early lead against Brighton Heights' hapless team. Though it was always a pleasure to see Seth play, the lack of suspense in the game gave Elissa plenty of opportunity to observe the action taking place on the sidelines and in the bleachers.

Andrew and some of his cohorts were pelting a group of junior high school girls with marshmallows, and the girls responded by squealing and gathering up the candy and tossing it right back. Not much game-watching going on there.

Aaron was standing as close as he could to the soccer team's bench, his gaze fixed on the field. Sometimes a player would speak to him, and his young face would glow with pleasure from the attention being paid him.

The cheerleaders were performing. This was the first year they'd been officially sanctioned to cheer at soccer games, and Elissa had helped them modify a few football and basketball cheers. She observed the routines and made a mental note to try something different. What they were doing wasn't working very well.

The cheerleaders did have one avid fan, however. Elissa noticed the small girl with long, dark pigtails right away. The child was watching every move the cheerleaders made and copying each one. She was a good little mimic and quite a gymnast too, Elissa noted, smiling. She could jump up and land in a split with far more grace and precision than the Petersen twins, the senior cheerleading co-captains, could.

And if her gaze happened to stray occasionally to Gray McCall . . . Well, that could not be helped. It wasn't as if she were gawking at the man, whom she had not seen or heard from since their aborted tryst in the hall. Aaron was standing down by the team, and she had to keep tabs on her little brother, didn't she? She glanced from Aaron to Gray, who was pacing back and forth with his usual intensity, his full attention on the game and his players.

No, not his full attention. A tall, strikingly attractive brunette had appeared out of nowhere and was pacing beside Gray, her lovely mouth curved in a playful smile. She tucked her hand into the crook of his elbow and gazed up at him with affection. Or was it adoration?

"Omigod, it's *her*!" Connie's voice sounded in Elissa's ear.

Startled, Elissa turned to face her friend, who had materialized as swiftly and unexpectedly as the brunette attached to Gray's side. "Who is she?" Elissa asked.

"I don't know her name or who she is exactly, but for the three years I've been at Riverview, that same woman has shown up at a few soccer games each season." Connie paused to breathe. "And it's very obvious that she's here to see the coach and not the team, isn't it? I hadn't seen her this term, and after I found you and Gray in the hall the other day— sorry, I won't mention it again—I assumed she was out of the picture."

It seemed that Connie had assumed wrong, Elissa

thought, feeling oddly winded. It was an unpleasant sensation, similar to what she'd felt the time her oldest brother, Tommy, had accidentally kicked her in the stomach during one of their rougher childhood games. Except back then she hadn't felt this dreadful psychic pain as well.

Her gaze flicked to Gray and the brunette. Certain things were starting to fall into place, though she didn't particularly like the picture they presented. No wonder Gray hated the fact that he was attracted to her and fought so hard against it. He was already involved with another woman!

"So he's not commitment-phobic after all," she said, hoping she sounded coolly amused when she was feeling anything but. "It appears he's committed to her." Pride kept her from showing, even to Connie, the pain and disappointment ripping through her.

Perhaps she wasn't as successful as she'd hoped, for Connie stared at her thoughtfully. "Maybe he's not committed to her, Elissa. Maybe he's still up for grabs. Look, if you want the man, go after him. Outmaneuver that brunette. I mean, it's been years and she hasn't bagged him yet. I'll be glad to help you plan your campaign strategy."

Elissa shook her head. "I appreciate the offer, and even though I know you're as shrewd a tactician as General Schwarzkopf himself, I'm going to decline, Connie. If I have to *bag* a man, like some kind of big-game hunter, then I don't want him."

"If you say so." Connie sounded doubtful. "But keep in mind, nothing's fair in love and war."

"I can't argue with that." She watched Gray stop his restless stalking and come to a standstill, his arm draped loosely around the brunette's shoulders.

Connie was watching too. "Do you really want to just sit there and watch her hang all over Gray?"

Gray was smiling down at the woman, who was saying something that clearly amused him. There was an intimacy between the two, so obvious that it hurt to watch.

Elissa purposefully looked away. "It's none of our business, Connie."

Shrugging, Connie moved on. Elissa walked over to the cheerleaders to give them a few pointers. The watchful, dark-haired girl listened intently, then approached Elissa.

"Are you the boss of the cheerleaders?" she asked, her brown eyes filled with respect.

Elissa grinned. "Well, I guess maybe you could say that. And I've been watching you cheer too. You do the straightest cartwheels I've ever seen, and your splits are fantastic. Mandy," she added, reading the name printed in multicolored stars on the little girl's T-shirt.

The child beamed. "I want to be a cheerleader." Her smile faded a little. "But my uncle says, 'Don't just cheer for the boys, play the game yourself.'"

Elissa nodded sympathetically. "It's a hard choice to make, isn't it? But sometimes girls do both, cheer and play. Not at the same time of course," she added, addressing that issue before it could be raised.

"That's what I'm going to do next year," Mandy said decisively. "Play soccer and be a cheerleader. When I'm nine."

"Good for you," Elissa said. Feeling benevolent, she called the Petersen twins over and suggested that the squad incorporate the little girl in one of their routines. The twins agreed and led the child off to join the others.

Several yards away, Jackie looked around for her daughter and saw her in the midst of the cheerleaders. "Oh my goodness, Gray!" she exclaimed, clutching Gray's arm. "Look at Mandy! She's cheering right along with the cheerleaders. They're even letting her call a letter."

Riverview was being spelled out vociferously by the

squad, and Mandy cartwheeled and shouted the second *r* as she landed on her feet.

"Isn't that sweet of them to include her?" Jackie was delighted. "Oh, I wish Paul was here with his videocamera to record it!"

Gray's gaze moved from the game to the cheerleaders, with whom his small niece was obviously having the time of her life. He vowed right then and there that he was going to purchase a videocamera himself. He and Jackie and Mandy had managed very nicely all these years with his 35 mm camera, until Paul Whittier had arrived on the scene with his state-of-the-art video equipment. And how Mandy loved watching herself on the reams of videotape that Paul was forever taking of her!

Gray frowned at the direction his thoughts were taking. He felt petty and resentful and ashamed of himself for it. Mandy liked her future stepfather, and Gray was glad of that. He wouldn't have wanted it any other way, but the little girl was all he had left of Gordon. He didn't want to lose her too!

His thoughts were too painful, too conflicting, and he swiftly turned his full concentration back to the game, though it had turned into such a rout that little coaching was required at this point. The next time his gaze flicked to the cheerleaders, Mandy wasn't with them. She had attached herself to Elissa Emory, and even from this distance Gray could tell Mandy was talking Elissa's ear off, as only a chatty eight-year-old can.

Elissa didn't seem to mind her small companion, though. She appeared to be listening and conversing, and even took the girl's hand at one point to guide her out of the way of a pack of boisterous junior high school students who'd swarmed down from the bleachers. The sight warmed him. Any kindness shown to Mandy evoked instant goodwill within him.

But as he continued to watch the two of them, the

heat being generated in his body had less and less to do with his avuncular feelings toward Mandy, and more and more with his decidedly lustful pangs for Elissa. And if he had any doubts that it was lust, his body was making it damn clear.

Gray felt the burgeoning surge of need, creating an almost painful pressure. But it was a kind of exquisite pain, mixed with anticipated pleasure so strong, he almost groaned aloud.

"I've got to sit down," he muttered, heading for the bench. Calling for some ice water, he slapped it on his face instead of drinking it. He would've liked to have doused himself with it. Just looking at Elissa made him hot as fire.

Deliberately keeping his eyes averted from that walking, breathing female danger zone, he turned his attention to the team, even though it meant ignoring Jackie. She didn't seem to mind, however. She was getting a kick out of watching Mandy hang out with her new friends, a pleasure Gray grimly denied himself.

When Aaron approached Elissa for money to buy a snack, she gave him extra to buy something for Mandy too. The little girl said she was hungry and there didn't seem to be anyone around to provide her with something to eat. Who'd brought Mandy to the game? Elissa wondered, as it neared the end and still nobody came to claim her.

The mystery was solved a few minutes after the game ended. The pretty brunette who'd been attached to Gray all afternoon approached Elissa. "I want to thank you for entertaining Mandy," she said. "She usually gets so bored during these games that we have to leave early. Not today, though, thanks to you."

"This is my friend Elissa, Mommy," Mandy piped up. "She's the boss of the cheerleaders and her brother is Seth on the team and her other brother is Aaron and he got me *this!*" She waved a roll of

Life Savers, the five-flavors kind. "I had so much fun today!"

Elissa was floored. *She'd been baby-sitting Gray's girlfriend's daughter? The two of them had been fully aware of Mandy's whereabouts all through the game and found it more convenient to let her stay where she was?*

Somehow Elissa's automatic, polite smile never wavered. "It has been fun," she said tactfully. Privately she thought that little Mandy deserved better than being foisted on a stranger so that her mother could devote herself to chasing Gray McCall. But then, as she'd told Connie, it was none of her business.

They made their good-byes, and Elissa watched Mandy and her mother make their way over to Gray. She quickly looked away. It was time to round up her brothers and go home.

It was past eight o'clock that night. Seth had gone to the library to study. "I don't know if Brenda is going to be there," he'd said indignantly when Elissa had inquired. "This isn't a ploy to get out of the house. I need to do my English paper."

Andrew was across the street at Bobby's house. "I don't have any homework," he'd said when Elissa had asked. "Nobody gave homework today, honest!"

Their father was working the swing shift till midnight at the airport, and Elissa was helping Aaron study his Word Wealth vocabulary-spelling list when the doorbell rang.

"*Dynasty,*" she read from the list as she rose to answer the bell.

"*D-i—*" Aaron began slowly. "*D-i-n-i-s-t-y?*"

"Do you think you could spell it without the *i*'s this time?" she asked wryly.

Aaron gave her a blank stare and Elissa suppressed a sigh. Her youngest brother seemed to have a natural propensity for misspelling. Either that, or this was the first time he'd looked at the list of assigned words.

"Try again, Aaron. Study the word and then write it five times. I'm going to see who's at the door."

She opened it to find Gray standing on the threshold. She was so surprised to see him, she was momentarily speechless. He was wearing the same clothes he'd worn at the game that afternoon, jeans and a blue shirt with a tie loosely knotted around his neck. She had changed clothes herself, and was wearing a comfortably oversized banana yellow T-shirt and loose-fitting cotton shorts.

"Hi." His voice was husky, his eyes hot and intense.

"Seth's not here," she said, finding her voice. "He's at the library working on his English paper."

"Good. Always glad to hear my players are keeping up with their classwork." Tense and unsmiling, Gray continued to stare at her. He waited for her to invite him in, but she didn't. Her expression was unreadable, and though her tone had been polite, her demeanor was guarded, even cool.

"So where's that monster dog of yours?" he asked casually.

"Jaws is in the backyard playing with his favorite toy, a Tupperware salad bowl. Do you want to see him?"

Gray cleared his throat. "Actually I came to see you."

"Me?" Her eyes widened with astonishment. "Why?"

"I wanted to thank you for being nice to Mandy this afternoon. She told me that you asked the cheerleaders to include her in their routines and that you bought her a hot dog and soda and candy. Both Jackie and I really appreciate your—"

"Jackie," Elissa cut in. "That's her mother?" Now

she had a name to put with the dark-eyed brunette. Gray and Jackie, Jackie and Gray.

Gray nodded in confirmation. "Mandy usually gets bored during the games and—"

"Yes," Elissa interrupted again. "Jackie told me." She considered adding, *Small children are often bored when they're left alone by the alleged caretakers in their lives,* but decided not to. "Mandy is a sweet little girl, and I enjoyed her company," she added instead.

Gray had no trouble believing that. He thoroughly enjoyed Mandy's company himself. Relaxing a bit, he found it easy to talk about his adored niece. "Mandy's already talking about coming to another game and cheering along with the cheerleaders. I'll record the whole routine on my new videocamera. I'm planning on buying one this weekend."

"That's nice," Elissa said flatly.

He shifted from one foot to the other. Elissa's responses were as impersonal as a stranger's, and he felt let down, disappointed. What the hell was he doing there? he asked himself, then wished that he didn't know the answer. Wished that he could delude himself into believing that he actually had come there to thank her on Mandy's behalf.

It didn't work. He couldn't believe the lie, not this time. The truth was, he was there because he couldn't stop thinking about Elissa, and the need to see her would not be denied. All through dinner that night with Jackie, Paul, and Mandy, he had been mentally absent, his mind on Elissa, his body throbbing from his provocative thoughts.

After he'd left the cozy threesome, he hadn't experienced the numbing loneliness that tended to strike when he considered the solitude of his own life. Images of Elissa had still filled his mind, leaving no room for anything or anyone else. Oh, he'd tried to spook himself out of his fantasies by telling himself that his obsession with Elissa was ridiculous, inconvenient, and even downright alarming.

Though he still fully agreed with that assessment, here he was on her doorstep, lamely blathering on about Mandy and videocameras. Meanwhile, his body, aching and hard, kept urging him to shut up and do something to relieve this wild sensual torment.

Elissa's perfunctory, guarded responses threw him off balance, though. She wanted him. He knew that. The way she had responded to him in the hall, before they'd been interrupted by the intrepid Connie, had left no doubt about that. But she seemed determined to play it cool now.

He was frustrated and disappointed; he didn't like playing games unless it was on the athletic field. Lily and her manipulative ways flashed briefly to mind. Usually a memory like that was enough to send him fleeing, but this time he stayed put. In Elissa's presence the specter of Lily faded into oblivion. It seemed that nothing could dampen the desire that coursed through his body as he gazed at her.

He studied her luminescent blue eyes and the sensual lines of her beautifully shaped mouth. He knew exactly where the dimples in her cheeks were, even though they weren't evident now, because she was not smiling.

Elissa was aware of his scrutiny and more than a little unnerved by it. She knew she wasn't mistaken about the yearning, hungry look in his eyes, and the one furtive glance she'd cast over his whole body had revealed physical proof of his arousal. *What kind of game was he playing?*

Anger surged through her. She would not play the role of the Other Woman. Romantic triangles were not for her. Anyway, she was long past the stage of spinning deluded daydreams about herself and Gray McCall.

She squared her shoulders decisively. He'd said

that he had come over to thank her. She would take him literally and proceed from there. "Well, you've thanked me for looking after Mandy," she said in a brisk, businesslike tone. "And as I said, the pleasure was all mine. Thanks for stopping by."

Gray smiled grimly. So polite. But she might as well have told him to get lost, so obvious was her eagerness to have him leave. She started to close the door and, driven by pure emotion, he put his hand out to hold it open. He was not used to giving up, and refused to quit now.

"One more thing," he said. "Jackie suggested that the next time she and Mandy come to a game, we all go out for dinner together afterward. Would you care to do that sometime?"

"All of us?" Elissa repeated incredulously. "You mean the four of us—you, Jackie, Mandy, and me?"

Oh, wouldn't that be fun? she thought. She knew exactly what her role would be—keeping little Mandy out of the lovers' way. "I have an even better idea," she said dryly. "Why not just drop Mandy and me off at Chuck E. Cheese while you and Jackie go into Columbus for an adults-only dinner?"

"What?" Gray gaped at her, clearly startled by her reply.

Elissa's sense of humor rose to the fore. Gray really wasn't very good at concocting and carrying out schemes. In fact he was terrible at it. In spite of everything, she was amused. "Gray, I know what's going on here. It's not hard to figure out. You're about as subtle as a nuclear warhead."

"Oh, really?" His tone was forbidding, but she was undeterred. "There's no need for subterfuge. You want to be alone with Jackie, you need someone to look after Mandy, and after today I seem to fit the bill." She lifted her shoulders in an elegantly indifferent shrug.

Too bad she wasn't coaching drama instead of volleyball, she thought. As an actress, she was a force to be reckoned with. "I don't mind baby-sitting Mandy occasionally, just let me know when," she added blithely. Really, this performance was Academy Award material. "She can come here. I'm home with the boys almost every evening anyway."

Gray stared at her, stunned. Elissa thought he was lusting after Jackie, that he wanted to dump Mandy to be alone with her mother! The concept was so shocking, so profoundly unacceptable and inappropriate, it bordered on the obscene.

His twin brother's face appeared before him, as clearly as if Gordon were really there. He remembered Gordon grinning as he described the "incredibly beautiful, funny, smart, classy girl" he'd met in an otherwise deadly dull college history class. That girl had been Jackie, and from their first date there had never been anyone else for either of them. As for Gray, he had never looked at Jackie or wanted to. . . .

He blinked, focusing again on Elissa's face. She was watching him quizzically. His pulses thundered in his head as he lowered his gaze to her mouth. Her lips were sensually shaped and he stared at them as if in a trance. No, he had never looked at Jackie and wondered what her mouth would feel like under his, had never felt an irresistible urge to pull her into his arms and find out. Which was exactly what he was experiencing as he gazed down at Elissa.

"You don't understand," he murmured.

"I think I do." Elissa backed away from him. The way he had been looking at her made her feel weak. She should be ashamed for responding, she scolded herself. On the other hand, *he* was not entirely blameless. If she was feeling the sensual heat, it was because he'd turned it on. Deliberately.

"What sort of an ego trip are you on anyway?" she asked. "You not only want me as a baby-sitter, but you want me to want *you*, even though you have Jackie. You're a snake, Gray McCall!"

"You're so wrong that it's—" He was cut off in mid-sentence by Aaron's voice, bellowing from the other room.

"Elissa, listen to this! *D-y-n-a-s-t-y*. And I'm not looking at the book either!"

"That's terrific, Aaron," Elissa called back. "Go home," she said sternly to Gray, her eyes as icy as an arctic night. "I'm very busy."

For the first time ever she was positively eager to do spelling with Aaron. It was a diversion, and she was badly in need of one right now. Walking to the middle of the living room, she called out, "Now spell *license*, Aaron. And then *incense*."

Aaron belted out his versions, adding and transposing *c*'s and *s*'s and getting both words hopelessly wrong. Meanwhile Gray had made no move to leave. He'd followed her inside instead.

She glared at him. "I said, *good night*, Gray."

"No, you didn't. You said, 'Go home,'" he corrected her wryly. "Look Elissa, about Jackie—" He stopped speaking as a textbook came flying into the room, followed by a frustrated, furious Aaron.

"I hate this stuff!" he howled, kicking the book into the air. "Spelling is stupid! I don't even care if I flunk it!"

Gray and Elissa ducked as the spelling book whizzed past them, missing them by inches. It hit the wall and landed open on the floor, page-side down. "Aaron Charles Emory, that's enough!" Elissa exclaimed. "That book almost hit us."

"I didn't mean it to hit you," Aaron muttered. "It sort of flew there when I kicked it. I'm sorry." He looked at the floor. "I didn't know you were here, Coach McCall," he added, shamefaced.

"That was some kick, Aaron," Gray said. "For a minute there, I thought I was at soccer practice."

"I'm really dumb," Aaron continued woefully. "I can't do anything. I can't play soccer as good as Seth and Andrew, and I can't spell these stupid words and—"

"You can sit around whining and feeling sorry for yourself," Gray interjected bluntly, "or you can practice till you're good. Practice spelling and practice soccer and don't give up till you get it right, no matter how hard it gets or how long it takes. The concentration and determination you put into sports can be used the same way to succeed in your studies. That's what makes a winner, Aaron, refusing to give up and focusing on your goals. Concentrate on what you want and make it happen. If you do that, it'll only be a matter of time before everybody knows exactly what you're capable of."

His tone was so forceful, so positive and intense, that both Aaron and Elissa listened with wide-eyed attention. He seemed to exude a dynamic energy that made it impossible not to believe everything he said, not to feel inspired to run out and do exactly what he'd said.

"I'm going up to my room to study," Aaron said decisively. He picked up his book and headed up the stairs, two at a time.

"That was an attitude adjustment," Elissa said, staring thoughtfully at Gray. "I'm impressed. Do you think you could come into the locker room before our next volleyball game and talk to the girls? It's not so much what you said but *how* you said it."

"I'm banned from the games, remember?" he drawled. "I've been labeled too exciting for certain players to cope with."

He smiled at her and Elissa almost smiled back. His eyes invited her to. Instead she fought the urge. "Well, maybe I could get that speech of yours on tape, then," she said shakily.

She tried to work up the necessary anger to order him to leave again. After all, nothing had changed for her to allow him to stay. But the anger wouldn't come, only a pulsing, tingling excitement that built and grew, even against her will.

It was demoralizing to realize she was having as much difficulty coping with his machismo charisma as young Vicky. Taking a deep breath, she tucked a few loose strands of her hair behind her right ear in a quick, nervous gesture.

He reached out to tuck another silky strand behind her left ear. The familiar, affectionate gesture stunned them both. For several seconds they stood stock still, their gazes locked, Gray's fingers still wrapped around her hair.

"Before I leave, I'd like to clear my name," he said quietly. "You're all wrong about Jackie and me, Elissa. She's Gordon's wife."

Elissa's jaw dropped. "Gordon? Your brother?"

He nodded, and she felt a flush of hot crimson color her cheeks. Jackie wasn't Gray's girlfriend at all, she was his twin brother's wife! What an embarrassingly wrong conclusion she'd drawn! "And that makes Mandy your niece, of course."

"Mmm, you're quick. If only you'd used those sharp, deductive powers of reasoning of yours in biology, you might have been another Madame Curie."

"Wasn't she a chemist?" Elissa retorted.

"I was using her as an example of success in the scientific field. Specifically, she was a chemist and a physicist."

"Oh," Elissa said, feeling sheepish. Not about the late great Madame Curie, but about other things.

"Oh," Gray mimicked gruffly. His grip on her hair tightened. Whether he used it to propel her forward or she came of her own accord, neither could be certain.

However it happened, she was in his arms, pressed against him so tightly that she could feel every taut plane of his body. She was acutely aware of the burgeoning, virile strength of him pulsing against her. A glowing heat flamed deep in her belly, and she felt a secret, aching throb. "I . . . uh, guess I should apologize for insinuating that you're a two-timing snake," she whispered.

She sounded contrite enough, Gray thought, but he caught the teasing glint in her eyes, and exhilaration surged through him. He tried to remember the last time he'd felt so alive. He was like a kid in an amusement park, excited and dizzy from the rides and filled with an anticipatory glow of what was to come. "I'm waiting for that apology," he said huskily.

She gazed up at him. Her arms crept around his neck and her body arched into his. "Do you want it in words?" she murmured, her lips curving into a sexy smile. "Or actions?"

"Oh, baby!" He made a sound that was half-laugh, half-groan. "If I thought you knew what you were doing . . ." His hands slid over her, caressing her back through the soft cotton of her shirt.

She drew back a little to look up at him, her eyebrows arched. "What makes you think I don't?"

He gazed down into her laughing, challenging eyes and was lost. In that moment all his efforts to keep away from her, his steely self-control and the self-protective walls he'd built, were swept away by a tidal wave of need.

He'd wanted her from the moment he'd seen her on the soccer field, all grown up into an enticing, irresistible woman, and the intervening weeks had only intensified his desire and sharpened his frustrations. All that pent-up longing was released in a wild and raging surge of hunger that would not be denied another second.

His mouth came down on hers, hard and hot. She clung to him and met his passion with her own, parting her lips to deepen the kiss, welcoming his tongue with a sensual flick of her own.

Her breasts pressed against the solid strength of his chest, the tips tightening into hard buds. He felt heir pressure, and a shudder of desire racked him. He wanted to see her, to taste her. . . .

With a rough sound of passion, he slid his hand beneath her shirt, closing it over her breast. Through the lacy material of her bra, he palmed the softness, rubbing the nipple with his thumb.

Elissa clutched at him, drowning in a stormy sea of pleasure. She slid her hands over the bunched muscles of his back, learning the feel of him, exhilarating in it, and wanting more, much more. Her fingers paused at his leather belt, which kept his shirt firmly tucked into his jeans.

He lifted his mouth from hers and buried his lips in the soft curve of her neck. "You make me crazy," he said hoarsely, gliding his hands over her body caressingly, arousingly, wanting her more with every stroke. The feel of her small hands on him sent his mind, always so ordered and controlled, splintering, ceding to the force of his passion.

She looked up at him with glowing eyes, her mouth moist and slightly swollen from their kiss, her lipstick thoroughly kissed away. "It's only fair," she said softly. "You started making me crazy a long, long time ago."

She thought back to her schoolgirl crush and all those fantasies she'd entertained about the two of them, but the reality of holding him in her arms, of being held and kissed by him were better than anything her imagination had conjured up.

She writhed sensuously against him, rising on tiptoe to nibble on his neck. She wanted him with a passion and need she had never experienced before, and the urgency of it drove her every move. Her thighs encircled one of his, deepening the intimacy of their already intimate position. She felt lightheaded as a thick, syrupy warmth coursed through her, pooling in her abdomen, leaving her legs shaky and weak. Far too shaky and weak to support her. She didn't want to stand anymore, she wanted to lie down. . . .

Gray's mouth took hers again, and they kissed hungrily, fiercely, the kisses growing hotter and wilder, each one melding into another until it was impossible to distinguish a beginning or an end. His hands were in constant motion, touching and caressing her breasts and her waist and her hips, then audaciously lowering to cup her derriere. His fingers kneaded her through her shorts, finding and tracing the lines of her panties under the cloth.

She gasped as he wrapped his hands around the backs of her thighs and slid them up and down in an erotic caress. His fingers traveled higher, slipping under the cuffs of her shorts to touch the lacy silk underneath.

Abruptly he pulled his mouth from hers and removed his hands, stepping back to set her free. The sudden shock of his withdrawal was disorienting. Elissa's limbs were so rubbery and unreliable, she was certain she would fall. Instinctively she grasped his shirt with both hands to keep herself upright.

Sensing her need for his support, he cupped her shoulders with his hands. The intensity in his gaze made her quiver. "This has gone far enough, Elissa. If I don't stop now, I won't stop at all, and there's a kid upstairs."

She swallowed thickly. "Oh, God, Aaron! Y-You're right, I—I wasn't thinking."

"I know you weren't." His mouth curved into a slow, heart-shatteringly sexy smile. "Neither was I."

Responding instantly, she melted into him, sliding her arms around his waist and cuddling against his chest. "I can't believe this happened," she said sighing softly.

"It happened." He kissed the top of her head, then disengaged himself from her embrace. "But it isn't enough, Elissa. I want more. I want everything. Come home with me."

Six

"Come home with you?" Elissa repeated haltingly. "Tonight?"

"Right now." Gray's eyes were burning and his gaze slid over her, hot as black fire.

The rampant sexuality in that look made Elissa shiver with sheer feminine longing. She wanted to put her hand in his and let him lead her out of the room, to take her to his place—or anywhere!—where they could resume their ardent, fiery lovemaking. She wanted to, but she knew she wouldn't.

"Gray, I—"

"You want me, Elissa, you know you do," he said urgently. "And you have to know how much I want you." He caught both of her hands and carried them to his mouth, kissing first one and then the other in a romantic gesture that thrilled her. "Come with me, sweetheart."

His voice was velvety soft, coaxing yet masterfully promising. Still gripping her hands, he tugged her nearer, closing the small distance between them. He dropped her hands to clasp her hips, lifting her slightly to position her against the hard heat of his erection.

"Come, Elissa." His voice lost none of its intensity,

though he'd lowered the volume to whisper-soft. "
want you to."

Her eyelids fluttered shut as he kissed his way
along her jawline, finally reaching her lips. His
mouth toyed with hers, nibbling and teasing, until
she moaned, desperate for the feel of his lips. When
he finally kissed her the way she wanted, the way
she needed to be kissed, she surrendered completely, wrapping herself around him, her body aching with pleasure and desire and pure need.

A long while later he lifted his head. His eyes were
dilated and heavy-lidded, his mouth moist from the
long, passionate kiss. Elissa lay limply against him,
dazed and weak.

"Let's go," he said in a husky voice that was almost
as stimulating as his kisses. He took her hand and
started toward the front door.

She didn't move. She closed her eyes for a moment
and took a deep, shuddery breath. "Gray, I can't go
with you."

"Yes, you can." He reached for her again. "The
boys are certainly old enough to be left alone for a
while and—"

"Of course they are," she agreed, stepping away
from him. "But it seems to me we're rushing things.
I mean, going to bed before we've even had a single
date strikes me as moving way too fast."

"A date?" he repeated, as if he'd never heard the
word before.

"Yes, a date. It's when a couple goes to a movie or
out for pizza or even into Columbus to the zoo or a
show or some other big-city entertainment." She
tried to keep it light, which took some effort because
Gray was edgy and tense and clearly not in the mood
for lightness. He was in the mood for something else
entirely.

"I know what a date is, Elissa."

Sexual frustration gripped him so fiercely, it took
considerable willpower not to simply pick her up and

carry her out of there. Their caveman ancestors' tactics did have the advantage of dispensing with maddening conversations such as this. But he was a man of the nineties, enlightened and supposedly above primitive behavior.

Gray ceded to civilized mores, though rather grudgingly. "But I don't feel like going to a movie or the zoo tonight. I don't want any pizza either."

"Must you take me so literally?" Elissa was dealing with a roaring sexual frustration of her own that was shortening her fuse considerably. "By dating I meant getting to know each other and spending time together, building a relationship that's not based exclusively on sex. That's not so hard to understand, is it?"

"We already know each other. We've known each other for years."

She frowned. "Do you really not get it? Or are you deliberately being dense?"

"A little of both, I guess." He sighed heavily. "This is what I get for being spontaneous," he muttered, more to himself than to her. "I haven't acted on impulse for years, and the one time I do, the one time I don't stop to think and analyze and control the situation, what happens? I get lectured for being spontaneous and impulsive."

"If you're trying to make me feel guilty, it's not working."

"I wasn't trying to make you feel guilty, Elissa."

"Because one of us had to stop to think and analyze and exert some self-control for the both of us. And as far as spontaneity goes, I think responsibility comes first."

"Responsibility is more important than spontaneity." He grimaced. "I remember giving a similar version of that lecture to some of the kids on the team when they came to me for advice about their girlfriends. Now, at the ripe old age of thirty-four, I'm on the receiving end of it. A truly humbling experience."

His head was clear now, the fierce sexual tension draining from his body, leaving him feeling . . . well, drained. He wanted nothing more than to go home, turn on the television, and lose himself in Monday Night Football. Maybe he would do a few hundred push-ups while he watched the game.

"You're right, of course," he said, backing toward the door. "I was out of line and I apologize for rushing you into something that you didn't want."

"You don't have to apologize." Elissa ran a hand through her hair. What was going on here? She hadn't meant to run him off, though that was the message he seemed to have taken.

"It's not that you were out of line," she hastened to explain. "I wanted it." Blushing at her own bluntness, she rushed on. "I mean, I was just as caught up in—"

"In fact, it's a good thing we didn't let ourselves get carried away," Gray went on, as if she hadn't spoken. He was still moving backward to the door, and picked up his pace as he talked. "It would have been a huge mistake on both our parts, to let one impulsive act ruin our friendship."

She flinched. "Are you saying that tonight would've been a one-night stand and nothing more?"

He was now leaning against the front door. "I hadn't thought that far ahead. In fact, I wasn't thinking at all!" he exclaimed, exasperated. "None of this was premeditated. When I kissed you . . ." He swallowed hard. "Things got out of hand. I'm glad you kept your cool and—"

"In case you didn't notice, I did *not* keep my cool," she countered, her eyes flashing. "I wanted you as much as you wanted me."

A good thing we didn't let ourselves get carried away, he'd said. She decided she didn't like his revisionist view of their passion. "We were both carried away," she said firmly. "It was exciting and wonderful and we both wanted—"

"Look, we've talked enough about it," Gray cut in, a little desperately. He threw his hands up in an emotional, very un-Graylike gesture. "There's no reason to keep going on and on about—"

"We haven't talked at all! We haven't even begun to touch on what this is all about."

"You know, Elissa, you don't just beat a topic to death. You bury it six feet under." He opened the door and stepped out onto the porch, not bothering to conceal his eagerness to escape. He detested analytical, soul-baring conversations. Having one with outspoken, hold-nothing-back Elissa was truly something to avoid. He thought of Lily's long, icy silences and decided that right now he would appreciate that treatment from Elissa.

Alas, she was not going to indulge him with frozen withdrawal. Instead she followed him out onto the porch. "Why are you acting this way?" she demanded. "Why are you leaving?"

"What am I supposed to do? I asked you to come home with me and you said no. In my book that's my cue to go home—alone."

"Well, *I* didn't give you that cue. I said I wouldn't go home with you, but I didn't ask you to leave." She gazed up at him. "Come back inside, Gray," she said softly. "We need to talk."

"Elissa, listen to me," he said roughly. He wanted to run from the emotional intensity reflected in her beautiful eyes. "You and me . . . it's just not going to work, I can see that now. You want a relationship, and I want—"

"If you say 'cheap, meaningless sex,' I'll brain you," she warned, fixing him with an exaggeratedly stern look of teacherly disapproval.

Disarmed, Gray couldn't help grinning. Elissa did have a talent of bringing humor into seemingly unfunny situations. "Sex could never be cheap or meaningless with you, Elissa."

"Ah! Do I detect another spontaneous remark?" She smiled at him, looking so warm and appealing that he was tempted to give in to her, to take her hand and go back inside and talk about whatever subject she felt like beating into the ground.

He successfully fought the temptation. He was thinking clearly and he was in complete control. Responsibility before spontaneity, he reminded himself. And responsibility meant honesty. "Elissa, I have to go. It's better this way, that we . . . uh, just stay friends."

"Friends," she echoed flatly. "You mean like—"

"I mean friends, not lovers. It can't be any other way."

She rolled her eyes heavenward. "Are you using reverse psychology, or something? I said I wouldn't go to bed with you until we knew each other better, and now you're telling me that you don't want me on that level anyway? And you know what's really strange? It's working. Your strategy is actually working! I want to argue with you that we *should* become lovers. At this rate I'll end up dragging you up to my room tonight to prove how good it'll be between us."

"I wish." He laughed, then sobered immediately. "No, now that I've thought things through, I realize what a mistake it would be for us to become . . . er, sexually involved. It wouldn't be fair, our expectations are too different. I don't intend to become seriously involved with anyone again, Elissa. I don't want the demands or the disappointments all of that entails. You want a whole lot more than I'm able to give, so let's preserve our friendship by not taking things any farther."

"Again," she said thoughtfully. "You said you don't intend to get seriously involved *again*. I take it that means you've tried it before."

"Tried and failed miserably." As much as he hated

talking about his brief, disastrous marriage, he felt obliged to explain his position to Elissa. "I was divorced eight years ago after a marriage that lasted twenty-one regrettable months, the last fourteen of which were pure hell. No." He shook his head. "Marriage just isn't for me."

"You mean, a bad marriage isn't for you."

"I mean, I don't ever want to get married. I like my life just the way it is."

"Wow, she must've really done a number on you." Elissa gazed at him curiously. "What exactly did she do to turn you into a loner for life?"

His lips tightened. "I'm not going to go into all the gory details, Elissa. It was over eight years ago, for Pete's sake!"

"Exactly. So why hang on to all the bad memories? Why let them influence your life today? You said yourself it was a long time ago. It's time to forget and get on with your life, if you ask me."

"Well, I didn't ask you," he snapped, and turned to leave.

She followed him down the porch stairs. "So, just because you married the wrong person and got hurt, you're shutting yourself off from ever experiencing happiness with anybody else? That's the stupidest thing I've ever heard. And the most cowardly."

"You don't understand!" Stung, Gray stalked down the front walk. "I don't know why I ever thought that you might."

Elissa was right at his heels. "I understand that I liked kissing you," she said hotly. "I understand that you liked kissing me too. And I understand that we could—"

He stopped and whirled around. "Will you just let it drop?" he said vehemently. "I have never met *anyone* as tenacious or as stubborn as you!"

She looked chagrined. "I've heard that before," she admitted. "My father says I'm as stubborn as a goat and as tenacious as a pit bull." She turned to walk back to the porch.

Gray was astonished by the wave of anger that crashed over him. Her father's characterization of her infuriated him. Never mind that he'd almost said the same things himself, he couldn't stand to hear anything negative about her from anyone else. "What kind of a man is your father to insult you that way?" he called after her, wondering if he sounded as irrational as he felt.

She stopped and marched back to face him. "Daddy didn't mean to insult me. I was probably driving him nuts at the time. You certainly know how that feels! And my father is very outspoken. He says exactly what he thinks."

"A trait that runs in the family, I see."

She frowned. "Which trait? Driving people crazy or being outspoken?"

"Maybe the two are linked," he said dryly, feeling calmer now, "in a kind of genetic string. You know, the way hair color and eye color are linked."

"Always the biology teacher." She sighed dramatically. "No, I never did quite get how hair and eye color are linked, though you tried hard to explain Mendel's law of inherited characteristics. One time I actually had a nightmare featuring those mind-boggling little charts about blood types."

"I have distinct memories of you and that standard lab experiment where the students test for their own blood type. According to your results, your blood did not fall into any of the four human types. Which are?" he prompted, suddenly smiling at her.

"A, B, O, and AB," she retorted. "You didn't think I'd remember, did you? Well, I do. I also remember that after I'd convinced myself that I was an alien with Blood Type Z, you did the test yourself and found that I was plain old Type O, the most common blood type of all."

Gray gazed down at her, enjoying the challenge

and humor that gleamed in her eyes. His blood quickened. He was attracted to her. And, he thought grimly, she knew it and used it well. Remembering how lusciously soft she'd felt in his arms took his breath away. *Friends,* he reminded himself a little desperately. They were fated to be nothing more than friends: It simply couldn't be any other way.

He cleared his throat. "Friend to friend—" he had to say it, he couldn't stress it enough—"I'm curious about something, Elissa. Along with the insults, does your father ever express his gratitude to you for giving up your own life to come back here and take over the family and the pets and housework and the yard work and—"

"You're making me sound like one of those down-trodden, self-sacrificing martyrs who turn up on TV talk shows to weep about how unappreciated they are." She shook her head. "I'd rather be compared to a goat or a pit bull. At least they have some spirit."

"Oh, you've got plenty of that, all right."

"Obviously too much for you. Isn't that right, *friend?*"

She'd moved closer, and they were standing toe-to-toe, staring intently at each other, an almost palpable tension vibrating between them.

An ear-splitting yell punctured that tension, startling Elissa and Gray so much that they both jumped. "What the—" Gray began, but paused when the cry became a distinct word.

"Lissssssyyyyy!"

"It's Andrew!" Elissa exclaimed, recognizing his voice at the same moment that she spied her younger brother running into the street. She ran toward him.

They met on the edge of the sidewalk, Gray right behind her. Andrew was holding out his right hand, and even in the dim glow afforded by the streetlight halfway down the block, Elissa could see the blood. In fact all she could see was blood. It covered the boy's entire hand and fingers, running down his arm and dripping onto his clothes.

"Andrew! Oh, Andrew, what happened?"

Before Andrew could speak, his friend Bobby was beside them, his eyes round with fear and worry. "It's all my fault," Bobby wailed, then added quickly, "but I didn't mean it. I was being stupid, but I didn't think he'd make a grab for it!"

"Here, let's wrap this towel around your hand, Andrew." Bobby's mother, Nancy, had followed the boys and began binding a thick towel around Andrew's bleeding hand. "Oh, Elissa, this is terrible!" she went on, sounding distraught. "We're so sorry. You see, the boys were downstairs in the basement and—"

"I was holding my dad's new knife," Bobby cut in, his voice shrill with anxiety and regret, "and I threw this apple up into the air. I wanted to try to slice it into pieces as it was falling. You know, like in the movies."

"It wasn't his fault," Andrew said, sounding dazed. "I thought the knife was a stick and that he was going to try to hit the apple like a baseball. I wanted to try it first, so I grabbed the stick. Except it was the knife and I grabbed it by the blade."

"He grabbed it real tight and it cut him real bad," added Bobby. "There's blood everywhere!"

"Andrew, press down with the towel to stop the bleeding," Nancy said. "Oh, Elissa, we're so sorry."

"Andrew, don't apply pressure," Gray said, slipping his arm around the boy's shoulders. "Just hold that towel against the cuts to absorb the blood. Hard pressure could damage the nerves and tendons if they've been cut."

Elissa stared at Andrew's bloody hand and the towel that was quickly turning dark red. She blinked, feeling lightheaded. "We'll go to the hospital right now," she heard herself say. Her voice sounded strange and faraway. "Bobby, would you run inside and tell Aaron where we're going?"

"Sure!" Eager to be of assistance, Bobby raced inside.

"I'll drive you," Gray said, already guiding Andrew toward his Jeep Cherokee.

Aaron, Nancy, and Bobby insisted on coming along, so they all piled into Gray's car, everyone talking at once. Everyone but Elissa, Gray noted as he drove to nearby Riverview Community Hospital. She sat silently in the front, with Andrew half on the seat and half on her lap, holding the towel around his bleeding hand.

They trooped into the emergency room, which was blessedly uncrowded and Elissa, Andrew, and Gray were quickly ushered into a treatment room. No one questioned Gray's presence there. It seemed as logical for him to accompany Elissa and Andrew as it was for Nancy to remain in the waiting room with Aaron and Bobby.

The nurse removed the towel and began to mop the blood with gauze pads. Elissa looked at the concentric cuts deep in her brother's palm and fingers and felt nausea surge through her. She was unaware that she'd swayed until she felt Gray's arms around her, holding her firmly, supporting her.

"You'd better wait outside," he murmured into her ear. His warm breath rustled her hair.

She watched the doctor and nurse examining Andrew's hand, and heard her brother gasp with pain. "No, I want to stay here," she said, reaching out to touch Andrew's shoulder.

"You're a pretty fair shade of green," Gray whispered. "I think you're about to faint."

"Lissy, it hurts!" Andrew cried, glaring accusingly at the doctor.

"I know, honey, I know." She squeezed his shoulder. "I'm right here." She closed her eyes for a moment, willing away her queasiness, consigning her dizziness to the far recesses of her mind. She felt a slow suffusion of color in her cheeks, and turned her head to meet Gray's eyes.

He was still holding her, and their faces were very close. "I'm all right," she said quietly. She reached down to remove his hands from her waist, but his fingers immediately intertwined with hers, exerting a subtle force that was strong enough to hold her in place. She was too preoccupied with Andrew's plight to exert her independence and push Gray away. Besides, it was useful having him there, because he talked to the doctor using medical lingo that she was unfamiliar with, eliciting information that she knew she wouldn't have been privy to on her own.

It was also comforting to lean against him while the doctor sewed up the cuts with so many stitches that she lost count. While the doctor concentrated on his handiwork, Gray kept up a running commentary with Andrew, about soccer, about football, about Jaws and school and myriad other subjects, successfully distracting him from staring anxiously at the surgical needle.

Andrew protested mightily when he learned that his hand had to be casted to his elbow. The doctor shrugged and proceeded to apply the cast while Gray explained the necessity of immobilizing his hand to keep the stitches intact. "You can't keep the thumb immobile without immobilizing the wrist too," he added.

"But I'm a starter on the junior high soccer team," Andrew said. "Can I play with this thing on my arm?"

"Absolutely not," the doctor said. "No phys. ed. class either. No sports for three weeks, until the cast comes off."

"*Three whole weeks!*" For the first time Andrew looked ready to cry.

"Three weeks with no sports is an eternity to a kid as active and competitive as Andrew," Elissa said to

Gray later that night as they sat at the kitchen table drinking decaffeinated coffee. Aaron and Andrew were both in bed and finally seemed to have settled down for the night. "He can't even play his video games unless he learns how to do it left-handed."

"Well, remember what that frighteningly cheerful nurse at the hospital told him. 'Now you can catch up on your reading, sonny.'"

"And did you see the expression on Andrew's face? Reading is not high on his list of priorities unfortunately." She took a sip of her coffee. "Oh, Gray, I still can't believe it happened. Bobby trying to slice an apple in mid-air like he'd seen in a cartoon and Andrew grabbing the blade with his bare hands. . . ." She shuddered. "Kids do the stupidest things."

"You won't get any argument from me on that. It's a great example of why a loaded gun should never be anywhere a kid can get his hands on it. Can you imagine if Bobby had had a gun instead of a knife and Andrew had made a grab for it?"

Elissa shivered again. They were silent for a few minutes, then she said, "I want to thank you for going to the hospital with us. It really helped, having you there."

He swirled his cup around, staring at the dark liquid. "I'm glad I could be of some use." He had felt useful, he admitted to himself. He'd felt needed and irreplaceable, as if he definitely belonged there with them. He was feeling that way now, sitting here with Elissa.

He jerked upright, startled at the revelation. Was that what he wanted? To be needed? To belong to—

No! He rose to his feet. "It's getting late," he said briskly. "Since the kids are asleep, I'll be on my way."

Elissa glanced at her watch. It was nearly eleven. Still, she didn't want him to go. It felt so comfortable, so *right*, sitting there talking to him. She made a stab at prolonging his stay.

"Gray, I haven't had a chance to tell you that your

first aid was first rate. The doctor said that applying pressure to Andrew's palm would have caused tendon damage, just like you said. It was nice having someone to serve as interpreter to the medical staff. You really spoke their language, gleaned from all those biology courses of yours, I guess."

"Actually, I took advanced anatomy and physiology classes back when I was in med school," Gray said, then cursed himself at the slip. She was certain to pursue it.

"You went to medical school?" she asked, right on cue.

He shrugged. "For two years. Then I quit."

"Oh."

"Yes," he said harshly, "I quit medical school to become a high school teacher and soccer coach. And, no, I didn't flunk out. I was in the top quarter of the class. But I quit and took the necessary education courses to qualify me to teach. Then I applied and was hired by Riverview."

He didn't wait around for her reply. He left the kitchen and walked swiftly to the door.

She followed. "'Night, Gray, and thanks again," she said quietly as he opened the door.

He gave her a hard stare. "Aren't you going to ask me how I could give up a promising, lucrative career in medicine to teach high school?"

"Is it a big mystery? I assume you decided that you didn't want to be a doctor. I can certainly understand that. I'd hate it myself."

Gray thought of his and Gordon's ambitious plans, to become physicians and share a practice, to be rich, respected, and well known, with all the accompanying privileges and entitlements. Gordon's illness had changed all that, making Gray realize for the first time that it had really been Gordon's dream, not his own. Gordon had always been the leader, the "outgoing twin" to Gray's "quiet twin." But it was more than that. Loving and admiring his brother so much, Gray had always gone along with Gordon's schemes and dreams and plans.

Everything had changed with Gordon's illness. Seeing his twin suffering in the hospital, having to deal daily with pain and death, had had a profound effect upon Gray. He'd realized that he wanted an entirely different kind of life. Without Gordon there to enjoy it with him, even the allure of a luxurious lifestyle lost its appeal. Lily, however, had not shared his newfound perceptions. She had already been angry at the amount of time he was devoting to his dying brother and distraught sister-in-law, and the prospect of being a mere teacher's wife had sent her packing for good.

Until now, he'd told no one in Riverview about his radical change in life plans all those years ago. Now Elissa Emory knew, and there she stood, accepting his decision as a rational one, not condemning, not really understanding. . . .

"You make everything so simple!" he muttered.

"No," she said mildly. "It's you who makes everything so hard."

"Not true. I'm a coach, a jock. Everybody knows we're easy and uncomplicated."

"Oh, I know the stereotype. I live with it. My brothers fit the mold, especially Seth. But not you, my friend. You're the most complex man I've ever met."

"You expect me to debate you on that?" he laughed uneasily. "Hey, I can't seem to get out of here. Every time I try to leave, I get drawn into a conversation or a spelling lesson or an accidental knifing or something equally compelling. Well, no more." He ruffled her hair. "This is definitely good night, Lissy."

The diminutive seemed strange coming from him. So did the avuncular pat on the head. She frowned. "Look, Gray, I can accept that you just want to be friends. You don't have to treat me like a preschooler to create even more distance."

She was way too perceptive, he thought. She could call him on things before he was even aware of what he'd done and why. "I don't know what you mean," he said stiffly, knowing exactly what she meant.

Of course, she went on to explain. "The fond pat on the head, the affectionate nickname. I bet you use the same tone and gesture when you're talking to your niece."

As a matter of fact he did. "That's it," he said tautly. "I'm out of here." He strode down the front walk, heading blindly for his car.

Seth met him at the gate. "Hi, Coach!" He looked and sounded guilt-stricken. "I . . . uh, I know it's late, but I had to go to the library and then I went over to Brenda's while she typed my paper for me and—"

"Get yourself to bed, Emory," Gray ordered in stern, coachlike fashion. "You keep burning the candle at both ends and our season will go down the tubes."

"Yes, sir!" Seth exclaimed, and hurried to the house, where Elissa still stood in the doorway. "I can't believe he came checking up on me again!" Seth said to his sister. "Jeez, Lis, I know I'm supposed to be keeping training hours, but I can't get to bed early every night. I gotta have some time to spend with Brenda!"

They both watched the taillights of Gray's Jeep Cherokee disappear into the distance. "You're going to have to be careful of your hours, Seth." Elissa smiled. "Because I have a feeling he'll be back."

"You mean like a hunch?" Seth gulped. "Your last hunch was right on target," he added nervously.

"The one about you and Brenda? That was sheer woman's intuition."

"And sheer woman's intuition is telling you that Coach McCall will be coming over again? Soon?"

Seth did not look happy at the prospect. Having his coach underfoot would cramp his off-the-field style.

"That's right, Seth." Elissa stared out at the dark, starry sky, and a small tremor of anticipation ribboned through her. "I think Coach McCall will come calling again very soon."

Seven

"Wow, she's right again! Women's intuition is awesome!" was Seth's greeting to Gray when the coach turned up at the Emorys' door the next evening.

Gray was accustomed to odd non sequiturs from students and had learned long ago not to try to figure them out. "How's Andrew's hand?" he asked instead. "I've been thinking about the poor kid all day, and since I was down at the track for my usual run, I thought I'd stop by and inquire about him."

Seth grinned slyly. "Yeah, right, Coach."

Gray froze. "What do you mean by that?"

The sharpness of his tone wiped the smile from Seth's face. "I didn't mean to be disrespectful, sir," the boy said quickly. "But since we're playing one of our biggest games of the season tomorrow—Holy Ghost Prep is undefeated and gunning to be division champions, too—I figured you were checking to make sure I wasn't out late tonight. And I'm not. See, I'm right here! I'm going to go to bed early, too."

Gray relaxed, smiling wryly. "Good, Seth. Glad to hear it. But I really am concerned about Andrew's hand."

"It's hurting him some," Seth said. "He stayed home from school today. Luckily our dad is working swing shift till Christmastime, so he was here with Andrew till Lissy got home at three. She gave him another one of those pain pills before she went out."

"Your sister's not here?" Gray struggled to sound casual, though the fierce disappointment shooting through him was anything but.

"Nah, she's out with some guy."

"Oh?" Gray barely managed to choke out the word. Elissa was *out with some guy?* He was staggered. And furious with himself for being so. "Who's the guy?" he asked before he could stop himself.

Seth shrugged. "I think he said his name was Josh. He's a pilot."

"An airline pilot?" Gray immediately conjured up a dashing figure in a uniform, with movie star looks and a platoon of female admirers. And Elissa was out with him.

Seth shifted restlessly, then cleared his throat. "Uh, Coach, have you already checked to see if Ben and Jeff and Phil and the other guys aren't breaking training?" Subtlety was not Seth's strong suit. Having passed this particular probe, he clearly expected his coach to take his inquiries elsewhere.

Gray had already decided to leave. There was no reason for him to stay.

He was saying good-bye to Seth when Aaron ran into the living room, an excited Jaws prancing at his side. "Peep's gone!" Aaron shouted. "He flew outside when me and Jaws came in the back door!"

"How did the bird get out of its cage?" Seth asked.

"I—I guess I forgot to close the door of the cage after I cleaned it." Aaron was crying now. He grabbed Seth's arm. "You have to get Peep, Seth. He has to be here when Mom comes back home!"

Seth uttered a blistering expletive, then turned to Gray, real anxiety in his eyes. "Peep is our mom's bird," he explained hastily. "We've got to find him. We can't tell Mom we lost her bird."

Gray sighed, bowing to the inevitable. "Do you

want me to help you look?" Although where one looked for a runaway canary at dusk was a question he'd never considered before.

At that moment Andrew, wrapped in a robe three times his size, came barreling down the stairs carrying a dripping-wet plastic trash bag. "I tried to tape this stupid bag around my cast to take a shower," he said, close to tears. "But it wouldn't stick and it fell off and now my cast is all wet. I hate it!" He hit the cast with his fist, then punched the wall with it. "I'm going to bust it off."

"This is no time to go mental on us," Seth snapped. "The damn bird is loose outside. You have to help us look for him."

"Peep is lost?" Andrew howled. "What'll we tell Mom?" He rubbed at his cast and gulped back a sob. "My hand really hurts, Seth. I shouldn't have punched the wall with it."

"I can't deal with all this!" Seth exclaimed, glancing wildly from one younger brother to the other. "Everything is going wrong! Why'd Elissa have to go out with that jerk tonight of all nights?"

"Calm down," Gray said, taking charge. "It's nothing we can't handle if we keep our wits about us. Seth, get a dry bag and tape it around Andrew's cast so he can shower. Aaron and I will go out and look for the bird."

Gray and Aaron headed to the backyard, where darkness was swiftly descending. "Aaron, I saw your bird fly into Mrs. Yoder's yard," called a young neighbor girl, whose backyard connected with the Emorys'.

"Oh, no!" Aaron gasped in horror. "Mrs. Yoder has three cats! What if they catch Peep and eat him?"

"We aren't going to let that happen," Gray promised.

"Mrs. Yoder lives three houses down," Aaron said, breaking into a run. Gray followed, along with some of the neighborhood children, who'd become caught up in the drama of the bird's escape.

"I saw him fly up into that tree," one of the children said, pointing to the towering oak tree that dominated Mrs. Yoder's backyard. Three fat cats sat in the grass watching the goings-on with supreme indifference.

Gray decided on the spot that the cats were no threat. Those overfed felines were not going to expend the energy to climb the massive oak, not for any bird. He realized that he, however, was expected to do so. The children, especially Aaron, were watching him expectantly.

A helpful Mrs. Yoder appeared to take her cats inside, then handed Gray a cracker spread with peanut butter to use as bait for the avian fugitive. Gray looked up into the thick, leafy branches, took a deep breath, and boosted himself up into the V of the trunk. . . .

An hour later it was all over. With Peep safely back in his cage, Gray and the three Emory brothers sat in the living room feasting on chocolate chip cookies, a victory treat provided by kindly Mrs. Yoder. Jaws was stretched out on the floor in front of the sofa snoring.

"It was awesome how high Coach climbed," Aaron told his brothers. "And when his foot slipped on that branch, right before he grabbed Peep, we all thought he was gonna fall. Mrs. Yoder even screamed."

Gray remembered the misstep, thirty feet or so above the ground. "I can't believe I was moronic enough to climb that tree, especially in shorts," he said, glancing down at the scratches on his arms and legs. His running shorts and T-shirt had offered little protection against the sharp scrapes of the branches. "I strongly recommend that you guys not try it, no matter what you're wearing."

"You're a hero, Coach McCall," Andrew said. "Mom really loves that bird, and you saved him."

"Yeah," Seth said. "Too bad Elissa missed all the excitement, going out with Jake? John? What's that guy's name anyway?"

"Jerk!" Andrew said exuberantly.

"Ah, yes, Jerk the glamorous airline pilot," Gray said.

The three boys hooted with laughter, and Gray joined in. The fraternal camaraderie was interrupted a few minutes later by the sound of footsteps on the front porch. Jaws sprang to attention and raced to the door, barking.

"Elissa's back!" Aaron said, jumping to his feet. "Wait till we tell her about Peep."

Gray glanced at his watch. She was back from her date at nine fifty-two? He was considering the implications of that when Andrew flung open the door. Elissa was waving good-bye to a man who was hurrying down the porch steps.

" 'Bye, Jeff. Thanks again," she called cheerfully.

"Jeff!" Seth snapped his fingers. "Oh, yeah, that's his name."

Aaron and Andrew fairly dragged Elissa inside, both talking at once. "Coach McCall climbed Mrs. Yoder's tree and rescued Peep?" she repeated incredulously, after getting the gist of their tale.

Elissa stepped into the living room, and her eyes immediately connected with Gray's. He was seated on the sofa, immobile as a stone.

She gave him a brilliant smile. "Well, this is certainly a surprise."

"Yeah, isn't it?" Gray swept his gaze over her. She was wearing a stylish denim jumpsuit and looked lithe and sleek, but softly rounded in all the right places. And she'd just come in from spending the evening with another man. His mouth tightened. The thought of another man touching her . . .

Gray drew a deep, steadying breath. The thought was unacceptable, and he immediately blocked it.

"So how'd the evening with The Boyfriend go?" he asked coolly. "Back kind of early, aren't you?"

So this was how he was going to play it? Elissa thought. Withdrawal, indifference. The perennial Mr. Cool. She decided his sarcastic questions had been a declaration of war, and walked over to the sofa. Sitting down beside him, she turned slightly, so that her knee touched his bare thigh. He looked at her sharply but did not move.

"Jeff's not my boyfriend, he's my movie friend," she said sweetly.

Gray scowled. Her blue eyes were bright and dancing, and he had the unshakable, unmistakable feeling that she was laughing at him.

"Jeff and I both love movies," she went on, "even the offbeat ones. Maybe especially those. Since they're never booked into Riverview's theater, we have to go into Columbus to see them." She tucked her legs under her, causing both her knees to press more tightly against his thigh. Her smile, her eyes, gleamed with challenge.

Gray settled deeper into the sofa, creating a dip in the cushions that shifted her even closer to him. If she'd expected him to bolt upright and flee, she was in for a surprise, he thought smugly.

"You only went as far as Columbus?" he asked, feigning nonchalance. "Why doesn't Mr. Airline Pilot fly you off to distant capitals to view these artsy, grandiloquent films in the cities of their origins?"

"Grandiloquent?" She laughed. "Aaron, do you think you can spell that one?"

"No way!" Aaron said. "Gran-dil—I can't even say it."

"Grandiloquent," Gray said smoothly. "It means pompous, bombastic."

"It better not turn up on my Word Wealth list," Aaron said darkly.

"Hopefully not," Elissa said. She glanced at her watch. "It's ten, guys. And it's a school night. Which is why I'm home early," she added, flashing Gray an innocent smile.

"C'mon, Aaron, Andrew, time to hit the sack," Seth said. "I'm going to bed, too, Coach. Gonna be well rested before the big game tomorrow," he added, seeking praise.

"Wise move, Seth," Gray said, but his attention was focused on Elissa. Hers was on him. Neither glanced away from each other as the three boys trooped out of the room and upstairs, and the brothers, engaged in a discussion about the upcoming soccer game, weren't even aware of the tension sparking between the couple.

"Who's this airline pilot you're referring to?" Elissa asked. She reached out to trace a long scratch on Gray's arm; it ran from his elbow to his wrist. "Did you do this getting Peep down from the tree?"

Gray shrugged and carefully removed her hand from his wound. He didn't need her sympathy. "You know damn well who I'm talking about. Jack or Jake or whatever his name is. Your movie friend."

"Jeff? He's not an airline pilot. He works for a marketing firm in Columbus but lives here in Riverview. He was a couple years ahead of me at Ohio State."

Gray shrugged again. "Seth said he was a pilot." He was not displeased with the man's change in employment. Working for a marketing firm simply didn't have the panache of flying jets all over the world.

"Jeff was talking to Seth about taking flying lessons. Maybe that's where he got the pilot idea. Seth doesn't pay much attention to things that don't specifically concern him. Even then they have to interest him or he doesn't really listen."

"I'm well aware of that. I had to teach him biology last year. He almost made you look like a prodigy in the subject."

"Uh-oh. I can sense where this discussion is

headed. Next you'll launch into another vivid description of my less than brilliant performance in your hallowed biology class. Time for me to go."

She started to rise, but Gray was too quick for her. Before she could move more than an inch, he clamped one arm around her shoulders and manacled her wrist with his other hand, effectively keeping her in place.

She arched her brows. "Then again, maybe I'm not going anywhere."

"No, you're not." He lowered her back against the cushions. "After all, this is what you intended when you cuddled up with me here on the sofa." His eyes challenged her to deny it.

She didn't. Instead she lifted her hand to stroke the firm line of his jaw.

"Your date didn't kiss you tonight," he said, his voice deep and low. He traced the shape of her lips with his thumb.

"How do you know?"

"Because I know what you look like when you've been kissed, and this isn't it." His mouth angled closer to hers. "Lipstick untouched and intact. Hair unmussed, not a single strand out of place. That's not how you looked last night."

"Last night," she repeated huskily, remembering.

His arm tightened around her, bringing her against his hard chest. Her breasts were crushed against the solid muscular wall. They were so close, there was nowhere else for her to put her arms but around his neck.

"Last night you said we could only be friends," she reminded him, even as she slipped her thigh between his. She pressed her mouth against his neck.

"Yeah, that was the plan, wasn't it?" His hands smoothed down her back, kneading along the length of her spine, then gliding over the curve of her hip.

"How does that saying go, something about the

best-laid plans of mice and men?" Smiling, she rubbed her lips against his.

"I can't remember it either." Gray was tired of talking, tired of thinking too. His mind was clouded with passion and his body throbbed with need. Neither condition was conducive to conversation or thought.

Instead he took action, doing what he'd spent most of the previous night and all of that day dreaming about. His mouth took hers in a hot, wild kiss that went on and on, getting hotter and wilder with every passing moment. Elissa arched into him, instinctively fitting her soft curves to the hard planes of his body. They seemed to be a perfect fit, two complementing halves joining strength and power and passion to form an inseparable whole.

They kissed again and again, deeply and passionately, their mouths, their hands demanding and possessive, their caresses becoming ever more ardent, more intimate. It took the sharp ring of the telephone to rouse them from their intense absorption in each other.

Gray reluctantly lifted his mouth from hers, his eyes glazed with sensual hunger. He stared at her, and the sight of her mouth, swollen from their kisses, the rose-tinted lipstick rubbed off, was evocative and arousing, making him want to reach for her again. He ran his hand through her tousled hair. "Now you look kissed."

She swayed toward him, her lips parting, her eyes drowsy with passion. The phone rang on. "Ignore it," Gray said. "Maybe whoever it is will give up and go away."

"But the ringing will wake the boys." Her sigh was part resignation, part regret. "Anyway, it might be my father on his break, calling to ask about Andrew's hand. He'll worry if there's no answer, and he'll keep calling till he gets one." Sighing again, she stood up.

Feeling extraordinarily possessive and giving in to the urge to be near her, Gray followed her into the kitchen.

"Oh, hello, Jeff," she said into the receiver. "No, I haven't gone to bed yet."

Gray stopped in his tracks. *Jeff?* The man who'd taken her to the movies? A sickening surge of jealousy sent him reeling.

"Oh, yes, I enjoyed it too." Her voice was light and friendly. Gray's expression turned stony as granite. "Of course, it always takes me a few minutes to get used to reading the subtitles, but then—"

The connection was abruptly broken. Gray stood in front of Elissa, his hand pressing down the bar on the phone. The muscles in his jaw were knotted with anger.

Elissa, still clutching the receiver, stared at him. "You hung up on him." She stated the obvious, clearly astonished.

"You're damn right I did. Did you expect me to patiently wait around while you entertain other men on the phone?"

"I wasn't entertaining anyone. I merely answered the phone and was being polite to the person on the other end."

"To the *man* on the other end."

"But you had no right to hang up on him." Her scowl was as fierce as his as she firmly replaced the receiver.

Gray jerked his hand away. He had a feeling she would've sandwiched his fingers in there if he hadn't. Hot color suffused his neck and spread to his cheeks. This was his first fit of jealousy. Even as the adrenaline pumped through his veins, a part of him wondered what on earth he was going to do next.

He had the opportunity to find out seconds later when the phone rang again. "If it's that marketing movie freak," he growled, "tell him to—"

"I'm not going to be rude to Jeff. Give me a minute to find out what he wants and then I'll—"

"Oh, I know what he wants! And it's not to sit in some cramped movie theater watching some incomprehensible foreign film while scarfing down Raisinets. He wants to take you to bed, baby, make no mistake about that!"

The phone continued to ring.

"That's not true!" Elissa cried. "Jeff and I are old friends who happen to share a common interest. But maybe you can't grasp that because your sole interest in me is sexual! I'm not a person to you, I'm simply a body!"

The ringing stopped, immediately followed by Seth's bellow from upstairs. "Elissa, it's for you."

She snatched up the telephone receiver. "Hello? Yes, we must have been cut off, Jeff." She glared defiantly at Gray as she spoke.

He turned and stalked out of the kitchen. Stifling a wild urge to tackle him, to pin him down until he apologized for his atavistic behavior, Elissa turned her attention to her caller.

"Remember those birthday cards you bought at the gift shop next door to the theater?" Jeff asked. "You left them in the car."

"Oh, that's right, I did." She stretched the phone cord as far as it would go, trying to get a glimpse into the living room. Even pulled taut, it wasn't long enough. She couldn't see Gray.

"If you need them right away," Jeff said, "I could drop them in your mailbox tomorrow on my way to work."

"That would be nice, Jeff. Thank you." They exchanged good nights and hung up.

"Jeff called to tell me I forgot the birthday cards I bought tonight," she said rather righteously, walking into the living room.

She was looking forward to Gray's chagrined expression, to watching him eat a full serving of the

metaphorical crow. Most of all, she wanted to hear
him deny the accusation she'd flung at him—that
she meant nothing more to him than an outlet for his
sexual urges. She really didn't believe such a thing,
she *knew* he must care.

Elissa stopped dead in the middle of the room.
Gray was nowhere to be seen. She called his name
softly, tentatively. He didn't respond, but Jaws
dragged himself off the big easy chair and came to
stand loyally by her side.

Elissa crept quietly upstairs, peering into her
brothers' rooms, even her own bedroom. She did not
find Gray in any of them. He was gone.

He'd walked out without saying good-bye! She gave
a hoarse cry of mingled hurt and rage. How dare he
treat her that way. She reviewed his sins: dropping
by at his own convenience, arousing her to a fever
pitch, then insulting her character by implying that
she was a manipulative tease who would play one
man off against another. And finally, worst of all,
leaving her. Rudely walking away as if she were some
worthless piece of trash who didn't deserve even the
common courtesy of a good-bye.

Elissa wanted to cry; she wanted to give him a
piece of her mind. She opted for the latter. Gray's
unlisted telephone number was printed on Seth's
team roster sheet that hung on the refrigerator. She
raced downstairs and impulsively called him.

Gray, who'd arrived at his house only moments
earlier in a foul mood, was tempted to ignore the
ringing telephone. He'd had it with phones! But after
letting it ring five or six times, he had second
thoughts. What if it was Jackie or Aunt Kay? Or
maybe one of the kids on the soccer team with some
kind of emergency? Sighing, he picked up the receiver.

"I knew you were there!" Elissa roared across the
line. "I was going to let it ring all night until I smoked
you out. What you did tonight was inexcusable, and

I'm not going to simply let it pass. You were rude and crude and—"

"You called to tell me how rotten you think I am?" he asked coolly.

"Yes! And to tell you that I hate the stupid, manipulative games that you play and that I'm through indulging you in them."

"I don't play games," he said, his reignited jealousy displacing his detachment. "You're the one who—"

"*I'm* not the one lurking in *your* neighborhood, pretending that I'm there for any other reason but the real one. I'm not the one setting limits on my feelings and then making up excuses to break them. You're the games strategist, Coach McCall, and I'm sick and tired of it."

She had to pause to breathe, but forged ahead before he could marshal a defense. "Okay, you had a bad marriage. Maybe your ex-wife was first cousin to the Wicked Witch of the West, but that doesn't give you the right to punish me. I refuse to pay for her sins, whatever they may be. I'm not some scheming little tramp and I won't let you treat me like one. I want you to stay away from me until—until—"

Elissa paused, her extemporaneous diatribe faltering. She wished that she'd taken the time at least to gather her thoughts before calling, but unfortunately a mental rehearsal was the antithesis of a heated, spur-of-the-moment act.

Gray took instant advantage of the lull. "It'll be my pleasure to stay away from you," he snapped. "Permanently!"

Lurking in her neighborhood! He was still smarting over that one. Because it was true, it stung all the more. He had been lurking in her neighborhood, pretending he wasn't there strictly to see her. But never again.

Elissa slammed down the phone hard. The tears she'd been holding at bay streamed from her eyes, and she angrily wiped them away. The man was impossible and she was *not* going to cry over him!

The banging sound was still reverberating in Gray's ear as he mounted the narrow stairs of his condo. He was as much shocked by her accusations as he was angered by them. Elissa couldn't be more wrong. He didn't play manipulative games. Nor had his behavior that night been rude or inexcusable. *Her* behavior had justified his every action, from hanging up on that Jeff creep to walking out. *She'd* been the rude one, not him.

He was the good guy, everybody knew that. It was the pernicious Lily who excelled in mind games of denial and deceit. Gray McCall was honest and open, straightforward and sincere. Why, Jackie was always praising his goodness. He knew she would be more than willing to give a testimonial on his behalf to Elissa. Not that he wanted her to.

His flirtation, or whatever it was, with Elissa Emory was over. He knew it was for the best. The kind of relationship she wanted—expected!—would be too disruptive to his routine, too intrusive to his privacy, too emotional for him to deal with.

Yes, this was definitely for the best. Having decided that, he refused to consider why something so essential to his well-being should make him feel so miserable, so very bleak and alone.

"And . . . Oh yes." The words came back to her, and she gathered the girls around for the finale. "We have to concentrate on what we want and make it happen. If we do, it'll only be a matter of time before everybody knows exactly what we're capable of."

"I think everybody already knows," Adrienne said grimly. "That's why they're laughing at us."

"Let's accentuate the positive," Elissa urged. "We're—"

"Poor Miss Emory, you're really trying hard to coach us," Laretha interrupted, putting an affectionate arm around Elissa's shoulders. "I wish we wouldn't keep letting you down, game after game."

"You're not letting me down," Elissa said, touched by the tribute. "Let's all agree to try harder, me as the coach and all of you as the team."

While the girls were showering and dressing, Elissa noticed a window propped open in the back of the locker room, providing an unparalleled view of the goings-on within to whomever passed by. A past scandal flashed to mind: During her sophomore year a group of enterprising student photographers had positioned themselves at that same open window with cameras, then attempted to sell the revealing photos to raise funds for a Photography Club trip.

Grimacing, Elissa hurried to the back to close the window. The volleyball team did not need that kind of publicity! She stood on a bench and was pulling the window closed, when hushed girlish voices drifted back to her.

"Well, tonight's the night!"

"You're really going through with it?"

"You're crazy, Vicky. I don't know what you see in him anyway. The man is old enough to be your father."

Elissa remained stock still. The tall rows of lockers concealed her from the girls, and them from her, but she recognized Vicky Drayton's impassioned, slightly hysterical voice. "He's only seventeen years older than me," the girl said defiantly. "That hardly counts at all."

"Coach McCall obviously thinks it does," Shannon retorted. "He doesn't want you, Vicky. He thinks of you as a silly little kid, if he thinks of you at all."

"I personally think Coach has something going with Miss Ware," chimed in Donna. "I saw the two of them walking down the hall together the other day and they looked pretty tight."

Elissa's lips twitched. Wait till Connie heard that one! She knew for a fact that her friend was currently beguiled by a thirtyish attorney ("he just could be Mr. Right, Elissa!") whom she'd recently met at a party in Columbus. ("I almost didn't go to that party, Elissa. I changed my mind at the last minute. It was Fate!")

"Gray thinks of me as a kid and a student because he's never seen me outside of school." Vicky's high-pitched voice pierced Elissa's reverie, and she tuned back into the girls' conversation. "He's never had the chance to know the real me. But tonight he will. He'll see me for what I am—a woman!"

"But your plan is so lame!" Rachel said. "To drive near his place, let the air out of one of your tires, then go to his house to use the phone to call for help. That's totally bogus, Vicky. He'll see through it in a minute. You'll make a total fool of yourself."

"You haven't heard the rest of her plan," said a disapproving Shannon. "She'll be wearing a raincoat, see, and when he comes to the door, she'll fling it open—"

"And flash him?" Donna squeaked in horror.

"I'll be wearing black lingerie," Vicky said. "Bra, bikini panties, garter belt, stockings, high heels, the whole works. Gray will *not* be thinking about my car at that point."

Elissa's jaw dropped. What a devilish plan Vicky had concocted! One that posed serious trouble for Gray. Even if nothing happened—and Elissa was

certain he would never lay a finger on the girl—
Vicky's very presence at his house, her scantily clad
presence, was a career-wrecker, a reputation wrecker,
a trust wrecker for a teacher and a coach.

"Shhh! Here comes Adrienne and Laretha!" Vicky
was shushing the other girls. "They can't find out
because they'd probably go straight to Gray and blab
everything!"

Good! Tell them! Elissa silently urged, but the
other girls said nothing. The animosity that existed
between the trio of princesses—Rachel, Shannon,
and Donna—and the athletic pair of Laretha and
Adrienne did not lend itself to conversation, let alone
confidences.

What should she do? Elissa wondered wildly.
Should she confront Vicky, tell her she'd heard everything, deliver a stern lecture and then . . . Then
what? Vicky would be furious at her and more determined than ever to entrap Gray. At best a confronta-
tion here and now would probably only postpone the
girl's scheme.

Elissa stayed hidden in the back of the locker
room, considering possible courses of action, as the
girls left. She knew she had to warn Gray, to let him
know that Vicky's schoolgirl crush was leading her
to employ decidedly unschoolgirlish tactics.

The problem was, how should she tell him? Elissa
thought about it the whole way home. She and Gray
hadn't spoken since their fight, and she'd been
wondering if they ever would. The only contact between them had been a mutual glare in the teachers'
lunchroom earlier in the week. Otherwise, they had
studiously ignored each other.

Now she had to break the news that Vicky Drayton
was about to appear on his doorstep in full seduction
gear. It was a daunting prospect. It wasn't until after
dinner, when she'd finished the dishes and the boys
had taken off—Seth to Brenda's, Aaron and Andrew

to baby-sit little Jared Berman—that she faced the inevitable and called him.

"Gray, this is Elissa Emory," she said the moment he picked up the phone. "I have to talk to you about a—a—" Her resolve and her nerve faltered. "A serious matter," she finished, then grimaced at the melodramatic sound of it.

"I'm listening," he said in a voice she could neither analyze nor interpret. Was he being caustic, angry, calm, encouraging? His tone was so enigmatic, she didn't know.

Taking a deep breath, she told him exactly what she'd overheard in the girls' locker room. He didn't interrupt her, and was silent for so long after she'd finished speaking that she wondered if he was still on the line.

"You have to do something, Gray," she said hesitantly.

"I know," he replied, and she breathed a sigh of relief. At least he hadn't hung up on her.

"Do you have any ideas how to handle this?" she asked.

He laughed sharply. She took that to mean no.

"Well, I've given this a lot of thought and I do have a plan," she said slowly. "Would you like to hear it?"

"Oh, definitely."

"I think you should call some of the boys on the soccer team and invite them to your place tonight. Insist that they come over if you have to. When Vicky arrives at your door, their presence will act as a deterrent to her . . . uh, planned exhibition. And you'll have witnesses that nothing happened between you, should she decide to invent some sort of tale that it did."

Gray cleared his throat. "And that's your plan?" For the first time he sounded uncertain, even confused.

"Well, it will certainly thwart her tonight. "But . . ."

"But?" he prompted.

Elissa sighed. "But what if she tries again? You can't keep the soccer team at your place every night. And your going out tonight isn't the answer either, for the same reason. She'll keep trying till she catches you at home."

"She's that tenacious, hmm?"

"I'm afraid so. A young woman who's willing to go that far to achieve her objectives is a force to be reckoned with."

"I think I agree with you. So what are we going to do?"

"You'll have to totally discourage her," Elissa said. "Let her know that it's hopeless and that she doesn't stand a chance with you."

"And how do you propose I do that?"

"You could always tell her you're gay."

"You're getting a kick out of this, aren't you?" he said mildly. "You enjoy seeing me squirm like a bug on a pin."

"Please hold the biology-lab analogies. As for enjoying this, no, I'm not. I feel sorry for Vicky because she's so desperate and misguided, and I even feel sorry for you, sort of."

"Enough to help me find a solution to this problem?"

"Well, I do have another idea. Unfortunately it's similar to Vicky's plot, in that both sound like something straight out of a soap opera."

"Interesting that you both think along the same lines."

"Another crack like that and I'll hang up and leave you to your own fate."

"I don't think that's the answer," he said, his tone firm with resolve. "Tell me your plan, Elissa."

"I parked my car a block over so that Vicky won't know anybody else is here," Elissa said nervously as she stepped into the combined foyer–living room of Gray's townhouse condominium.

"Excellent attention to detail," he said approvingly.

Her gaze darted from him to her surroundings. "So this is where you live," she murmured, feeling the need to say something, anything at all.

"This is it. Come on in and make yourself at home."

She nodded, flashed an uneasy smile, and sat down on the wide, thick brown sofa. The room was furnished in spartan style, containing only the sofa, a hexagonal-shaped end table with a lamp on it, and another longer table that held a television set. The walls were painted a dull white, and there were no prints or pictures hung to enliven them. Clearly Gray McCall did not have much interest in interior decor.

Gray studied Elissa as intently as she studied his home. She was wearing a loose-fitting bright coral cotton dress that looked like an oversized T-shirt, and he wondered how she managed to make that shapeless sack of a dress look sexy. But she did. His pulses leaped, and for one distracting moment his mind went blank.

His mouth was suddenly dry. Was she in similar straits?" Do you want something to drink? Coffee, OJ, beer?"

She shook her head.

"Maybe later, hmm?" He sat down beside her on the couch, not too close, but not at the opposite end either.

She shifted uneasily, then stood and began to pace the silent, half-empty room.

Gray pressed a button on the remote control, and the TV set flashed on. "Is there anything you'd like to watch?" he asked politely.

"Whatever you want is fine with me." She peered out the wide living room window, which was bare of curtains or blinds or shades. "At least we'll have a clear view of Vicky arriving."

The sounds of the all-sports network filled the room. A college football game was being broadcast, but since it wasn't Ohio State, Elissa had no interest in it. She glanced covertly at Gray, still seated on the couch. She expected his attention to be glued to the TV; her father and brothers were instantly hypnotized whenever any game of any kind appeared on the screen. She was startled to find him staring at her instead.

She fidgeted, suddenly nervous again. "Maybe I will have something to drink, after all. You just stay there, I'll serve myself." She made a hasty trek through the minuscule dining room, which a round oak table and four chairs nearly filled, into the all-white kitchen. The contents of the refrigerator were as uninteresting as the rest of the place. She poured herself a glass of juice, sipped it, then set the glass down, grimacing.

"You don't like it?" Gray was leaning against the doorjamb watching her.

"How did you manage to mess up frozen orange juice? All you do is add water to the frozen concentrate and stir."

"You're not going to believe this, but I forgot to add the water. I was running late the other day and didn't bother to read the directions. I just threw the contents of the can into the blender and mixed it up." He shrugged. "I don't think it tasted all that bad."

"It does, trust me on that." She rinsed out the glass, refilled it with water, and gulped it down. "I wonder when Vicky will show up."

"Mmm, I wonder." He sat down at the kitchen table. Elissa remained at the sink, but her gaze kept drifting his way. He was wearing a pair of faded jeans that fit him well. She gulped and looked away. They fit him extremely well, defining all his masculine attributes. His gray and red Ohio State T-shirt looked old and comfortably soft, and did marvelous things for his muscular chest and arms.

"We really didn't get into the details of the plan over the phone," she said, striving to break the tension-filled silence that stretched between them. "Do you want to run through it now?"

He shook his head. "I don't feel like talking about Vicky anymore," he said, a bit impatiently.

"I . . . uh, understand that this must be somewhat awkward for you." She grinned suddenly. "It must be a terrible burden, being so incredibly irresistible that you have to plot and scheme to keep women from throwing themselves at you."

He stood up. "I hope you're prepared to pay the penalty for that particular personal foul." He walked toward her, looming tall and strong and menacing.

Except he wasn't menacing in a threatening way. He was menacing in an attractive, playful way, encouraging her to get sexily menacing right back. Elissa's stomach did a spectacular flip. She knew the inevitable outcome of this scene.

He would come close, very close, and she would reach out to give him a push, a push meant to entice him, not repel him, and he would recognize it as the come-on she meant it to be. He would catch her hands and pull her to him. They would gaze deeply into each other's eyes, and she would slowly, dreamily melt against him. . . .

Elissa drew a sharp breath and ordered herself to get a grip. Her imagination was becoming as overheated as Vicky's! Anyway, they'd played that scene before and decided . . . Her fingers clenched. Exactly what had they decided? It was probably irrelevant anyway, because she and Gray were champions of the mixed message, saying or doing one thing while meaning something else entirely.

She felt excited and confused, and she recognized both those states as signposts on the road to losing control. It happened so easily to her when she was alone with Gray. Far too easily.

Steeling herself, she squared her shoulders and

forced herself to meet his eyes. "Gray, you know why we're here." She tried to sound bracing and businesslike, reminding him of their common objective. Reflexively, though, she took a few steps backward.

He advanced toward her, smiling wickedly. "Yes, I know why we're here, Elissa." He did not sound at all bracing or businesslike. Instead, his voice was lazy and seductive.

She watched him warily and backed up some more. Too late, she realized she'd backed into a wall. The doorway from the kitchen to the small dining room was several feet to her left.

Gray took full advantage of her tactical error. He placed his hands on either side of her, caging her between the wall and his body. He seemed to tower over her, standing so close yet not quite touching his body to hers. His warmth, his size and strength, the clean soap-and-male scent of him filled her senses, arousing her with dizzying speed.

She pressed her head back against the wall and forced herself to avoid his intense eyes, fixing her gaze instead on the unyielding dullness of the opposite white wall. "Gray, I—I didn't come here for this," she said shakily.

"But here we are, together again," he murmured, nibbling gently, sensuously on her upper lip.

He slipped his thigh between hers, and she yielded to him, parting her legs to accommodate his hard male pressure, achingly aware of the devastating stimulation. But instead of protesting their intimacy, she felt a giddy triumph that she was back in his arms.

She could no longer concentrate on her focal point on the opposite wall, not when she was surrounded by the touch and feel of his intoxicating masculine strength. Her eyelids lowered. As if of their own volition, her hands rose to rest on his waist. He was going to kiss her, and she wanted it so much.

Their lips toyed with each other's, savoring the

contact, heightening the anticipation of what was to follow. Elissa sighed softly and arched into the welcoming heat of his body.

The sudden loud buzz that boomed throughout the condo was as disorienting—and unwelcome—as a kick in the head. Worse, the noise did not cease, but buzzed on incessantly.

"That must be Vicky!" Elissa exclaimed, gathering her shattered wits. She ducked under Gray's arm and headed for the door.

He followed, watching as she peered through the peephole in the front door. "It's Vicky, all right, and she's wearing a raincoat buttoned to the neck," Elissa said breathlessly. "Okay, time to put our plan into action."

"She's here?" Gray was standing still as a statue, his face a mask of horror. "You mean it's really true? Vicky Drayton is actually here, dressed or *undressed* as the case may be hoping to . . ."

"You didn't believe me?" Elissa asked indignantly. "You thought I made the whole thing up?"

He didn't have to reply, his expression said it for him. She was outraged. "Whatever made you think I would do such a thing?" she demanded, ignoring the ear-splitting buzzer. "Why on earth would I ever make up such a preposterous story?"

"I thought you did it to get things back on track between us." He looked at the floor, frowning. "We were in dire need of something to break the ice—it was reaching glacier proportions—and so I figured that you'd decided to—"

"As if I spent all my time and energy plotting ways to entice *you*!" Elissa was beyond simple outrage now. She'd ascended into the stratospheres of wrath. "You have an enormously inflated opinion of yourself, you vain, conceited—"

"Elissa, listen to me. I'm certainly not vain or conceited enough to believe that one of my students would deck herself out in a Frederick's of Hollywood getup and offer herself to me as a present to unwrap. That premise struck me as ridiculously unbelievable. Believe me, I do not have such grandiose delusions of my own appeal."

"But you had no trouble believing that *I* would plot and scheme and lie to get you alone! Why was that so easy for you to believe? Do I seem so pathetically desperate that I'd resort to cheap tricks to get your attention, especially after you'd made it quite clear that you don't want to have anything to do with me?"

"I believed it because I wanted it to be true," he said flatly. "I've hated how it's been between us the past couple of weeks, Elissa. No talking, no smiling." He reached out and caught her hand. "No touching."

"But you didn't mind it enough to do anything about it!" She wrenched her hand from his.

"I agreed to take part in your plan tonight," he reminded her.

Elissa was not mollified. "I ought to go home right now, sneak out the back door, and leave you to deal with Vicky on your own."

The buzzer continued to sound. Vicky was clearly intent upon gaining admittance.

Gray looked alarmed. "Elissa, please! You can't do that to me."

"All right. I'll stay and help you because I wouldn't put anything past Vicky, not even calling her father to catch her here undressed and alone with you. And then you'd probably be fired for contributing to the delinquency of a minor, and the soccer team wouldn't make it to the state finals without you coaching them, and my brother would be crushed." She folded her arms and glared at him. "That's the only reason why I'm doing this, and don't you dare presume otherwise!"

"At this point your wish is my command," he said dryly, earning himself another fierce glare from her.

She went to the door, then glanced back at him. "I hope you really do remember the plan."

"It isn't something I'm likely to forget," he said as he headed up the stairs.

Elissa opened the door. "Vicky!" she exclaimed in faux surprise.

Vicky gaped at her with genuine shock and horror. "Miss Emory! Wh-What are *you* doing here?"

Elissa smiled what she hoped was a mysterious, sexy smile. "Oh, I'm here quite often," she said, lowering her voice confidentially.

Before Vicky had a chance to react, Gray called from upstairs, "Who's at the door, sweetheart?"

Vicky blanched, then turned beet red when Gray appeared on the staircase, barefoot and tousled, looking as if he'd just climbed out of bed and pulled on the T-shirt and jeans he was wearing.

"Vicky Drayton is here," Elissa said, glancing from Gray to the nervous girl.

"I—I have a flat tire," Vicky said quickly. "I was driving and it . . . er, just blew out. I was hoping I could use your phone to—to call someone to change the tire for me."

"No need to call anyone." Gray sauntered down the stairs to stand directly behind Elissa. He wrapped both his arms around her waist and pulled her back against him. "I'll change the tire while you keep Elissa company here inside." He nuzzled Elissa's neck. "I'll be back soon," he murmured, loud enough for Vicky to hear. "You know I can't stay away from you for long, darling."

Elissa smiled weakly. They were working without a script, and she thought that Gray was definitely overacting. The plan had been for her and Gray to pretend they were seriously involved, thus ending Vicky's hopes for anything more than a student-teacher relationship with Gray. Gray, however, seemed bent on carrying things a little too far.

She wriggled out of his arms. "Where's your car, Vicky?" she asked, and the girl mumbled that it was parked down the street, the left-rear tire totally flat.

"I'll take care of it right away," Gray said. He planted a swift, hard kiss on Elissa's mouth and loped out the door without glancing once at Vicky.

Elissa felt a pang of sympathy for the glum young woman standing forlornly in the doorway. How terrible to be seventeen years old and in love with a man who didn't love you. She'd been there herself, with this very same man. Gray's appeal was potent indeed.

Still, Vicky's perfidy had to be dealt with. "Would you like a nice glass of orange juice, Vicky?" she asked, taking the girl by the arm and leading her toward the kitchen. "Why don't you take off your coat? You must be awfully warm."

"No!" Vicky clutched the lapels with both hands. "I'll leave it on."

Gray returned a short time later to find Elissa and Vicky sitting at the small kitchen table. Elissa was sipping water, while Vicky had managed to choke down half a glass of the appalling orange juice.

"The spare tire is on," he announced heartily. "Funny thing about that blowout, though. The tire appeared completely intact. Looked more like someone had deliberately unscrewed the valve and let the air out of the tire."

"I have to go home!" Vicky jumped to her feet and fairly raced out the front door. It slammed behind her.

Elissa stood up. "Well, mission accomplished, I believe. I had a little talk with Vicky, woman to woman."

Gray arched his brows. "I think I'm glad I wasn't around for that."

"Vicky won't be back to bother you again." Elissa sighed. "Unfortunately I don't think she'll be playing on the volleyball team anymore either. I'm not exactly her favorite person at this point."

"I'm the one she should be hating, not you."

"Maybe." Elissa shrugged. "Jealousy is not a rational emotion."

He grimaced. "How true. Some people have been known to make total fools of themselves when caught up in the throes of a jealous fit."

"Is that a fact?" She tilted her head to one side and gazed through her lashes at him.

"It is." He cleared his throat. "Elissa, about the other night . . . I ought to apologize. I guess I shouldn't've hung up on that jerk even though—"

"Jeff is not a jerk," she said succinctly. "And no, you shouldn't have." She glanced at her watch. "It's nearly ten. I'd better go. Andrew and Aaron will be back from the Bermans soon."

Gray heaved an exasperated sigh. "You're still mad, aren't you?"

"Your powers of perception are amazing, Coach McCall."

"Well, what are you mad about? The other night? Tonight? *Both?*"

"Truly amazing."

"I already apologized, Elissa."

"It was a paltry apology, and you didn't mean it anyway."

"Paltry?" His face reddened. "You're *rating* my apology? And how do you know whether I meant it or not?"

"I know you didn't mean it because you called him a jerk, and because you said you guessed you ought to apologize, which certainly qualifies things. Well, don't do me any favors, McCall. As far as I'm concerned, you can keep your precious cool and your meaningless apologies. I'm going home."

He watched her walk from the kitchen to the living room. She was leaving, and tomorrow they would be back to their nonsmiling, nonspeaking, nontouching impasse. Elissa really had come there that night to save his reputation, not to take up with him again. As he'd thought. *As he'd hoped!*

"Elissa, wait!" She stopped and turned, her hand on the knob of the front door. "I haven't thanked you yet," he improvised quickly. "For warning me about Vicky. For coming here tonight and—and helping me get rid of her."

"I told you why I did it," she said coldly.

"Yes, you did. For Seth and the soccer team."

"And for Vicky," she added virtuously. "She was playing a dangerous game and she needed to be set straight."

"And you're definitely the one to do it. When it comes to setting people straight, you are without peer."

Something in his tone put her senses on alert. She watched him approach her, acutely aware of the burning hunger in his eyes, of the throbbing power of his body. Sexual tension vibrated between them.

"Your thank-yous are as dubious as your apologies, Coach."

"So you rate thank-yous, too?" Before he could stop himself, he reached for her.

Elissa felt the controlled strength of his arms as he pulled her to him. She didn't resist. As her body impacted softly against his, Gray loosed a deep-felt sigh of relief. She wasn't going to push him away, she wasn't going to leave him. He held her tight, inhaling the enticing feminine scent of her, savoring the warm feel of her.

"Can we put all the misunderstandings and arguments and everything else behind us and start over?" His breath brushed the top of her head, his lips touched her silky soft hair.

She drew back a little and stared directly into his eyes. "Start over as what? As former student and teacher? As teaching colleagues? Or as friends?"

"How about all of the above?"

Her arms had been straight at her sides. Now she lifted them, laying her hands against his chest as she stood on tiptoe to deliver a quick, sisterly kiss to his cheek. "Consider it done. Good night, Gray."

She started to pull away, but he tightened his arms around her, physically forbidding her departure. "Why do I have the feeling we're in some sort of chess game and I'm about to get checkmated?"

"Do you?" She smiled up at him. "Are you?"

"You're good, Elissa. Tough. And did I mention supremely tenacious?"

"That's what makes a winner," she said brightly. "Refusing to give up and focusing on your goals. You have to concentrate on what you want and make it happen."

"Those are sound coaching principles."

"I know. And you can apply them both on and off the playing field."

"Let's try applying them now." He bent his head and drew her tightly against him. His mouth opened over hers, and she moaned when his tongue sought hers, tilting her head back to accept the power of the kiss, to deepen the intimacy.

Sweet, hot pleasure eddied through them both as they clung together, driven by a desire and need that multiplied a thousandfold every time they touched.

Gray covered her breast with his hand, taking possession, his long fingers beginning a slow, sensual massage. He rubbed her taut nipple, making her gasp with pleasure as fiery sparks of pleasure rebounded deep within the most secret part of her. She twisted feverishly against him. She felt empty and achy and needed to be filled. By him, only him.

She needed to be his woman. And she would be, she promised herself. She had to be patient, she had to believe. . . .

He jerked his mouth from hers, his hands still clutching her tightly. "I want you," he said hoarsely, throwing out all cool euphemisms and admitting the hot, unequivocal truth. "You have to know how much I want you, Elissa."

"I want you, too, Gray," she whispered, clinging to him. "I want us to be lovers." She felt a spasm shudder through him, and he lifted her up in his arms.

"Yes, sweetheart. Oh, yes! It's going to be so good. So good, baby, I promise." He started toward the stairway.

"Gray?" Elissa's voice sounded high and unnatural to her own ears. "How can I tell you this?" she went on. "I want us to be lovers, but . . . I didn't mean for it to happen tonight."

Nine

Elissa squeezed her eyes shut and braced herself, waiting to hit the ground with a thud. When she didn't, she opened her eyes and peeked at Gray's face. His expression was inscrutable.

"I thought you were going to drop me," she murmured. "Are you?"

"That would hardly be sporting." He slowly, carefully, set her on her feet, letting her slide down his body, deliberately pressing her against the thick bulge in his jeans. "Tempting maybe, but not at all sporting."

"And you are most definitely a good sport," she said softly, standing close to him.

She realized she was trembling with relief, for she had not wanted to argue with Gray again. If he had insisted, she knew she might have given in to him, just to keep from fighting. But he hadn't pressured her. He was willing to listen to her. "I've heard," she went on, "that you instill the virtues of good sportsmanship into your players. It's nice to know you live by your own rules, Coach."

"Yeah, I live by the rules, even though sometimes it's frustrating as hell. So while I'm focusing on my goal and concentrating on making it happen, why don't you explain your game plan to me?"

"My game plan?"

"You know, what we do in the meantime. While we're waiting to become lovers."

Elissa tried and failed to suppress a grin. "We could go out, spend time together, get to know each other really, really well. I think I explained the concept of dating to you earlier."

"Right, the movie-pizza-drive-to-Columbus routine. And after the requisite number of dates . . ."

"You are goal-oriented to the extreme, aren't you?"

"Hey, I'm simply focusing and concentrating, Elissa."

"Then it'll only be a matter of time before you show me exactly what you're capable of."

"Your locker-room talk really turns me on." He clasped his hand around her nape and guided her to the door. "But since the lady says, 'Not tonight,' I'll walk you to your car."

"Gray?" she gazed up at him. "Thank you." She paused, feeling emotional and terribly vulnerable. "Thank you for understanding."

A half-moon shone down on them as they walked along the narrow sidewalk, holding hands. They reached her car and stood beside it, both reluctant to part.

"You know that we have a soccer game tomorrow," Gray said, "but if you want to go out for dinner afterward . . ."

"I'd love to, but tomorrow is my father's day off. He'll be at the game and then . . . Well, Daddy likes a home-cooked meal and all of us there for it when he's home. Why don't you have dinner with us?"

Gray frowned. This was already getting complicated. Of course, he should have remembered that there was nothing simple in the minefield that comprised male-female interactions.

"Uh-oh, I can practically see the wheels turning in

your head," she teased. "You're wondering how to get out of this. Every instinct you possess is screaming for you to head for the hills."

He was spooked that she'd hit so close to the truth, but gamely tried to cover it. "As a native Ohioan you should know that there are no hills around to head to."

"We're having pork chops, applesauce, sweet potatoes, salad, and pie," she coaxed. "Conversation will be easy. All Daddy and the boys ever talk about is sports."

"Good food and solid conversation. When you put it that way, how could a guy refuse? I'll be there tomorrow around six, Elissa."

The dinner turned into a celebration of the soccer team's victory, and the menu and conversation were exactly as Elissa had promised. The Emory males were delighted with Gray's presence, and each vied for his attention. Gray was amused that none of them had a clue that he was there specifically to see Elissa. They didn't even catch on when she walked with him to his car as he was leaving. Since Jaws went along, Gray figured they thought she was taking the dog out for his nightly sabbatical.

"I should warn you," he said as they stood by his Jeep Cherokee and Jaws romped through a pile of raked leaves, sending them scattering, "that your dad told me he's off again tomorrow and he's already asked me over for dinner. Feel free to rescind the invitation."

"I wouldn't dream of it. Tonight my father was more animated and more like his old self than he's been since Mom's accident, and my brothers didn't fight once. I give full credit to you, Coach McCall. You fit in with them better than I do."

Gray smiled. He'd enjoyed himself, and the prospect of spending a similar evening tomorrow was a pleasant one. "Do you cook every night?" he asked. His solitary prepackaged, microwave-nuked meals and Jackie's perpetual spaghetti were light-years removed from what he'd been served at the Emorys' table.

"Sure. I started cooking with my mother when I was in kindergarten. It's never too early to learn, you know." She grinned at him. "The way to a man's heart being through his stomach and all that."

For the first time Gray truly appreciated the wisdom in that old adage. He leaned down and kissed her forehead, then headed for home.

Later that night, as she tossed and turned in bed, Elissa thought about that chaste, brotherly good-night kiss. Her imagination kept conjuring up images of her and Gray together, and the things they were doing were far, far removed from chaste and brotherly.

She had enough brothers and did not want or need another one. And though it was her own idea, being chaste with Gray was already murder on the nerves. She wanted so much more. But she also wanted more than the no-strings sex that he would certainly be willing to indulge in with her.

Focus and concentrate on what you want and make it happen. She knew what she wanted: for Gray to fall in love with her, because she was certain beyond a shadow of a doubt that she loved him. Making it happen was something else entirely. Would a man who'd given up on love ever let himself fall in love again?

"Elissa, are they true?" Connie demanded, plopping herself down on one of the chairs in the art room. The dismissal bell had just rung, liberating Riverview's students and teachers for the day.

Elissa was tacking up the environmentally themed

collages that her third-period sophomores had completed earlier. "Is what true, Connie?"

"All those wild rumors going around school about you and Gray McCall, of course. Don't tell me you weren't aware of them. *Everybody's* heard them. Why, the lady who dishes out the soup in the cafeteria line was talking about it with the salad server today at lunch."

Elissa grinned wryly. "Being the star of the latest hot rumor does have certain drawbacks. Everybody gossips *about* you, but nobody gossips *with* you." She glanced at her friend. "Exactly what's being said about Gray and me, Connie?"

"Oh, plenty. Which do you want to hear, the G, PG-13, R, or X-rated version?"

Elissa groaned. "I hope Gray hasn't heard anything. He would hate being gossiped about."

"Then you're really a couple?" Connie was thrilled. "I've been hoping for that ever since I saw you two together in the hall that time I'm never supposed to mention. What does it feel like to have your fantasy come true, Lissy? Because Gray McCall was your number-one fantasy in high school, and now you're—"

"Still fantasizing, Connie."

Connie's face fell. "Huh?"

"Gray and I have been spending a lot of time together these past couple of weeks," Elissa said, artfully arranging the collages and just as artfully avoiding Connie's eagle eyes. "He has dinner with us almost every night, usually at our house, but he's also taken the boys and me out for pizza a few times. Once we all went to the movies, one of those action-adventure flicks about cyborgs or something. It was terrible, but the kids loved it."

"What fun," Connie said with a definite lack of enthusiasm.

"Gray is absolutely wonderful with my brothers, Connie. He stayed with Andrew when he got the cast off his hand and is helping him with the physical-therapy exercises. He helps Aaron with his home-work and with his soccer, and he's had a number of serious, confidential talks with Seth—about Brenda, I think, though neither will tell me."

"That's cool for your brothers, but does he ever have any time for you?" Connie sniffed. "This is not the stuff of which hot rumors are made, Lissy. What kind of a fling is this anyway?"

Elissa's cheeks turned a deep pink as heat rippled through her. "Connie, I don't want a quick, hot fling with Gray."

"Well, of course you don't, but you do need some romance, don't you? Elissa, you can be straight with me. I know you want to marry Gray McCall. It's like he's your Destiny and you've known that since you were seventeen years old!"

Elissa winced. "It's not quite as simple as that, Connie." In fact the situation was growing impossi-bly complicated. *Some romance.* Connie had scored a perceptive hit there.

It had been her own idea to stay out of Gray's bed while they built a relationship based on something stronger and more lasting than sex. Now she worried that her good intentions had backfired. She and Gray spent so much time together and were so comfortable and easy with each other, she was begining to wonder if his sexual attraction to her had faded as he turned her into the sister he'd never had.

He never kissed her anymore. He never even touched her! Didn't he want to? Of course, they were rarely alone, but he didn't even take advantage of those times when they were. There were no more hungry kisses during stolen moments. He no longer even bothered to bestow one of those chaste pecks on her forehead. The last time he'd displayed any desire for her had been the night Vicky showed up with her tire ruse. Vicky hadn't been back to his place since, and neither had Elissa.

Didn't he want her anymore? she wondered constantly. The week before, Gray had been right there in the kitchen when Jeff had called to tell her about the new French comedy that had opened in Columbus. Remembering Gray's reaction the last time she'd gone out with Jeff, Elissa had been tempted to accept the invitation, strictly to see if she could provoke another jealous rage. To bait Gray into staking his claim on her in a very physical way . . .

Elissa sighed. She hadn't done it. She'd felt ashamed that such a manipulative scheme had crossed her mind, even for a moment, and had politely declined Jeff's invitation. Gray had heard her do so, but he'd said nothing, nothing at all.

"Lissy, sometimes Destiny needs a helpful push," Connie said. "I'm very good at providing ideas and momentum in such cases, and if you—"

"Hi, Elissa!" A small whirlwind in a pink jogging suit raced into the art room, followed by Gray McCall himself.

"Mandy!" Elissa gave the girl a quick hug. The two of them were good pals now. Mandy had spent the last three soccer games she'd attended with Elissa and the cheerleaders. Jackie had remained with Gray the entire time; he'd even been the one to fetch the little girl at the game's end. Elissa had waited for him to suggest that they all have dinner together, which he'd mentioned the night she had misinterpreted his relationship with Jackie. The subject never came up, though, and the dinner never came off. Elissa got to know Mandy quite well and the child's parent not at all. She tried not to let it bother her.

"Jackie needed an emergency sitter," Gray explained to Elissa now, "and pressed good ole Uncle Gray into service. She dropped Mandy off here, but I'm completely tied up with my research biology students in the lab. Then there's soccer practice at four. Do you think you could—"

"Mandy can stay here," Elissa said before he could ask. "We have a volleyball game against Freeport High at four, but she can come along with me."

"And watch the inevitable slaughter?" Connie said as she stood up. "Poor child. Lissy, think about what I said and remember, I'm available for whatever needs to be done." She swept grandly out of the room.

Gray watched her go, shaking his head. "I won't even ask what that was about. Undoubtedly something terrifying, knowing the audacious Ms. Ware. Thanks for the favor, Lissy. Mandy, honey, I'll see you later."

"Uncle Gray calls you Lissy, just like Aaron and Andrew do," Mandy said after Gray left.

Elissa smiled wanly. "I noticed that." She looked more closely at the little girl. "And I just noticed something else. Mandy, you got your ears pierced!"

Mandy beamed with pride. "Paul took me to the mall on Saturday. I've been wanting to get them pierced since I was five, but Mommy and Uncle Gray always said no. But on Saturday Paul—he's going to be my new daddy—said, 'Why can't Mandy have her ears pierced?' So then Mommy said, 'Okay, but I'm not going to watch,' so Paul said he would go with me. I was real brave, Elissa. I just said *ouch* when the needle stuck me, but I didn't jump or cry."

Elissa listened attentively till the end of the monologue, but the child's casually inserted phrase "he's going to be my new daddy" nearly drowned out everything else. Gray hadn't mentioned that his brother, Gordon, and Jackie were divorced.

"So now you'll have two daddies," she said carefully. She was both curious and confused and felt guilty for pumping an eight-year-old for information that was Gray's to supply.

"Sort of," Mandy said, picking up a piece of pastel chalk. She drew a large round smiling sun on the blackboard. "One daddy in my house and one daddy in heaven."

"In heaven?" Elissa repeated incredulously.

"My first daddy died," Mandy explained. "So he lives in heaven now and I'm going to have Paul for my next daddy. I always wanted a daddy to live in the same house with me, even though Mommy said it's special to have a daddy in heaven."

"Gordon is dead?" Elissa was thunderstruck. *Gray's twin brother was dead?*

Mandy nodded. "Gordon. That was my first dad's name. I can't remember him, but I know he looked exactly like Uncle Gray because they were twins, like those cheerleader twins, Polly and Patty."

Mandy chattered on, something about Polly and Patty looking like her Barbie dolls, while Elissa sank into a chair, speechless. She felt oddly bereft, for though she'd never met Gordon McCall, Gray had talked enough about his brother that she felt as if she knew him. She'd been looking forward to meeting Gordon, though she'd never suggested it, believing Gray would eventually get around to it. But that would never happen now. *Gordon was dead!*

Mandy was unaffected by Elissa's stunned silence. In fact she was totally oblivious to it. She did enough talking for the both of them while busily filling the blackboard with her chalk mural. Shortly before four o'clock a subdued Elissa and the loquacious little girl went to the gym where the volleyball team was gathered.

Only seven girls were left on the team. As Elissa had predicted, Vicky had quit the day after her fateful appearance at Gray's house. Her departure had not affected the hapless team's losing streak. Their string of defeats had continued, although they'd managed to score an occasional point now and then.

"Hey, Miss Emory, you got us a new player!" joked the Kovach twin when she spied Mandy.

"I can play volleyball," Mandy said. "But you have to show me how."

The Freeport team hadn't arrived yet, so Laretha, Adrienne, Bethany, and the twin took turns teaching Mandy the basics of volleyball. The other three girls pored over a copy of *Glamour* and Elissa sat on the bleachers, lost in thought. And all her thoughts were of Gray and Gordon McCall.

A stocky grim-faced man arrived at four thirty-five and introduced himself as the coach of the Freeport High School girls' volleyball team. "That is," he added, scowling, "I was the coach until this afternoon, when only four girls showed up for the game. This is the fifth game we've had to forfeit this season because they can't be bothered to play, and I've had it. I quit. I just drove over here to tell you that there won't be a game today. We forfeit and it's your win."

"Our win?" Adrienne exclaimed. "*We win?* Us? Our team has a win?"

"We won a game!" Laretha screamed. She and the twin grabbed each other and hugged. "No matter what else happens, we won't have a winless record for the season!"

The euphoria built, affecting everybody, even Rachel, Donna, and Shannon. After much squealing and hugging and high-fives, the girls left the gym, half delirious with glee.

Caught up in the ecstasty of it all, Mandy insisted on going to the soccer field to tell her uncle the wonderful news. "Our team won, Uncle Gray!" she shrieked as she raced along the track toward him. Having shared the historic moment of glory, she now considered herself a part of the team. "We won the game!"

Gray left a practice drill to join Mandy and Elissa on the sidelines. "The volleyball team won a game?" he repeated, astounded.

"And we didn't even have to play it!" Mandy added.

"Oh, so Freeport forfeited?" Gray smiled broadly. "That's not really winning."

"It's recorded as a win," Elissa said coolly. "And we'll take a win any way we can get one. You do realize that you've lost our bet, don't you, Gray? And according to the terms of the bet, you will be chaperoning the Fall Dance this Friday. And remember, because it falls on Halloween this year, it has a Halloween theme." She took Mandy's hand to lead her from the field. "I'm taking Mandy to my house now. You can pick her up there after practice."

"Since the other team forfeited, that means you didn't win the bet either," Gray called after her. "It also means I'm not chaperoning the dance."

Elissa didn't even look back, much less answer.

"I'm going to be a red crayon for Halloween," Mandy confided as she trotted alongside Elissa. "My mom made my costume. Paul is taking me and my friends trick-or-treating while Mommy gives out the candy at home." She dropped Elissa's hand to turn a cartwheel in the grass, talking all the while.

Mandy had a definite talent for filibustering, Elissa concluded. Nothing was left unsaid by her. She was as talkative and open as her uncle was close-mouthed and guarded. By the time Gray arrived to pick Mandy up, the little girl had invited herself for dinner and set herself a place at the table.

"Seth asked me to tell you that he's having dinner at Brenda's house," Gray said to Elissa when he entered the kitchen.

She nodded absently and went on mashing the potatoes. Gray watched her for a moment, frowning.

Mandy pounced on him. "We're having fried chicken for dinner tonight, Uncle Gray. Want me to ask Elissa if you can stay too?"

"You don't have to ask," Aaron said. "Coach knows he can eat over whenever he wants."

Still Elissa was silent. Gray cast a tentative glance at her, wondering why she seemed preoccupied and remote. She stayed that way all through dinner, though the children made up for her lack of conversation with a steady stream of their own.

In the middle of dessert—some sort of vanilla wafer and pudding concoction—Mandy blurted out, "Will you go to that Halloween dance with Uncle Gray, Elissa?"

Aaron and Andrew snickered. Gray smiled, nodding. "Elissa's going to the dance, Mandy. If I have to chaperone, so does she."

"Good," Mandy said. "Because I'm worried that you'll be sad on Halloween, Uncle Gray."

"Why would he be sad on Halloween?" Andrew asked curiously.

"Because Uncle Gray always took me trick-or-treating, but not this year," Mandy explained. "But it's okay because Uncle Gray can be with his girlfriend instead, right, Elissa?"

"Girlfriend?" Aaron echoed. His eyes widened. "Are you Coach McCall's girlfriend, Lissy?"

"Girlfriends are under twenty-five years of age," Elissa said grimly. "That makes me too old to be one."

"Is Uncle Gray too old to have one?" Mandy asked truly concerned.

"Hey, this is getting pretty personal, kids," Gray said. "Let's talk about something else."

"By all means." Elissa stood up and began to clear the table. "Let's be evasive and make sure that we keep everything on a superficial level so that nothing of importance is ever revealed." Her voice was tight, her tone tense and brittle.

The three children fell silent for the first time, glancing uncertainly from Elissa to Gray. "Are you going to have a fight like Seth and Brenda?" Aaron asked. "They're always fighting."

"There isn't going to be any fighting," Gray said. "Everything's just fine." He cleared his throat and attempted a wide, reassuring smile. "Say, isn't it almost time for the *Cheers* reruns? Why don't you kids finish your dessert in the other room, in front of the TV?"

"So you two can have a fight out here without us listening." Andrew grinned cheekily. "Sure, we'll get lost." He picked up his dish and left the kitchen, followed by a compliant, giggling Mandy and Aaron. Jaws, ever hopeful of a handout, dashed after them.

"What's wrong?" Gray asked the moment the three were gone. Elissa stood at the kitchen sink, her back to him, concentrating fiercely on scraping and rinsing the dishes before stacking them into the dishwasher.

"What could possibly be wrong?" she replied. "Everything's fine, you said so yourself."

He stared at her, baffled. "Are you angry about the bet? Because I didn't renege on it, Lissy. Technically neither of us won, so in all fairness, we both have to chaperone that dance. And you don't have to cook me any special dinner. I've already had so many of them here that—"

"I don't give a damn about the bet or the dance or the dinner." She marched over to the bird cage, dropped some morsels inside for Peep, stalked out the door into the small backyard. She stood there in the grass, rocking back and forth on her heels and staring up at the sky.

"Maybe you'd like to clue me in as to what's going on with you?"

She turned at the sound of Gray's voice. He was standing on the concrete slab that passed for a back porch, his arms folded over his chest. He looked confused and wary, and Elissa sensed he was deliberately keeping his anger in check.

She wished she had done the same, but it was too late now. She had exploded and he wanted to know why.

"You were edgy all through dinner," he said, coming to stand in front of her. "Even before that."

She shrugged. "I'm in a rotten mood. It happens sometimes." She silently willed him to pursue her, to *make* her tell him what was really bothering her.

Gray was not about to do so. The cool and aloof core of him, long sealed off from emotions and involvement, eschewed coaxing and delving into feelings.

"Okay," he said brusquely. "It's time for me to take Mandy home. I'll give you a call about chaperoning on Friday."

Elissa knew that as far as he was concerned, that was that. But not for her. "Gray, were you ever going to tell me that Gordon is dead?" she asked impulsively.

Her voice was low and soft, but Gray heard every word, and they stopped him in his tracks. He stood unmoving, as if frozen to the spot.

"You talk about Gordon a lot," she went on. "He comes up quite naturally in conversation, but you never mentioned that he happened to be dead. I was shocked when Mandy told me."

"Mandy told you," he echoed. He remained motionless, his posture rigid.

"What happened, Gray? When did he die? Mandy seems to have no real recollection of him, so I assume that—"

"Gordon died from a rare, fast-growing brain tumor eight years ago. Mandy was just an infant, so naturally, she has no memory of him."

"Eight years ago," Elissa whispered. "That was when you dropped out of medical school, when your marriage broke up, too." She knew without him saying so that Gordon's death was the catalyst for both.

"I didn't deliberately set out not to tell you, Elissa." He clenched his teeth so tightly, his jaw ached. "There just never seemed to be an opportune moment. It's so . . . It's too . . ." His voice trailed off.

"Serious? Personal? And we've kept everything light and fun between us?"

"Not always," he countered, surprising her. She had just given him the perfect out and was heartened that he hadn't taken it.

"We've talked about your mother," he went on. "You told me how worried you are about her and how hard it is to see her suffer. We've talked about your father and brothers and how they're adjusting. We've discussed problems with students. None of that is light and funny, Elissa."

"But even when we were talking seriously, you never brought up Gordon's death."

"No." He balled his hands into fists. A cold desolation seemed to seep into his every pore. He felt winded, as if he'd been hit in the chest with a wrecking ball and was staggering under the force of the blow.

"You said I'm evasive and superficial." He shrugged wearily. "Guilty as charged, I guess. Who can blame you for being furious?"

"Furious?" She clutched his arm and turned him to face her. "I'm so sorry about Gordon's death, Gray, so sorry. You've had so many losses, so much pain. But losing your twin brother . . ."

She broke off, gulping back a sob. She had heard the genuine affection in Gray's voice when he'd talked about Gordon. She instinctively knew that the loss of his twin had been devastating, hurting him so much that he still couldn't bring himself to talk about it. She could not imagine enduring such unbearable pain and loss. Gray had survived it, but the scars were deep.

She wrapped her arms around him and hugged him close, though he was unresponsive. It didn't matter. She simply held him tighter and cuddled closer. Her heart blazed with love for him. She wanted to heal him with the soothing warmth of her love, to melt the protective walls he'd built around himself.

"I wasn't trying to keep it a secret from you," he said at last. "I wanted you to know, I'm glad you know now."

"You just didn't want to have to tell me," she said softly. "I understand. It's easier for me to talk about Mom's accident to people who already know about it. Having to tell someone who doesn't know is difficult. Breaking the news, dealing with their shocked reactions. You get depressed all over again. I do understand, Gray."

He drew back and gazed down at her, his eyes dark and intense. "It's more than that, Elissa. You see, when we're together, I don't always think about Gordon. For the first time in eight years, he's not constantly on my mind. When I'm with you, I think about you and what we're doing and what we're talking about."

He gave a short self-deprecating laugh. "I believe it's called living in the present. Maybe it's simply called living. Whatever, I hadn't been doing a very good job of it, not until I met up with you again at the junior high track field about nine weeks ago."

"Oh, Gray," she whispered, cupping his face with her hands. She was so in love with him, and he needed her, she knew it. If only she could extend that need into love.

He was lifting his arms to embrace her when the kitchen door banged open and Andrew shouted, "Lissy, phone for you! It's your friend Jill in California."

Elissa closed her eyes and silently cursed the terrible timing. "Andrew, tell Jill I'll call her back."

But Gray had already moved away from her. She knew as she watched him stride swiftly toward the house, that for him the intensely emotional time of revelation was over.

She followed him, frustration coursing through

her. For those few precious moments, they had been so close, and for the first time Gray had opened up to her, revealing his thoughts and feelings. And he had been about to take her in his arms! After the long weeks of deprivation, she was starved for his touch. But they were back in the midst of the Emory family circus, the opportunity to end the famine lost. Her emotions were churning, her body radiating heat. It didn't help that Gray appeared calm and collected, the master of cool once more.

"California, hmm?" he said as they reentered the kitchen. "Sometimes I forget that you lived out there."

"I'm going back as soon as Mom can manage here at home without me," she said.

She'd cast a verbal gauntlet, but Gray did not pick it up. "How did you happen to end up in California anyway?" he asked.

The contrast between his current amused and detached self and the emotional, sensitive man he'd been just minutes ago was stunning, and Elissa had to suppress the urge to snarl in frustration. They were back to playing it his way; there would be no more information or talk of Gordon that night. Gray probably considered the subject closed for good.

He went on, teasing her. "Were you one of those pale little Midwestern girls who played Beach Boys records and dreamed of surfing on the beach? Did you always wish you could be a California Girl?"

"Not quite," she said testily. "Three of my sorority sisters planned to move there after graduation and they invited me to come with them. I'd never been out of Ohio and I decided it would be an adventure to go. And there was a man, of course." She threw him a defiant look.

"There usually is," he said mildly.

"My college boyfriend, Todd Merrill, had a job lined up in southern California."

"And? I assume the romance hit the rocks, as this

is the first mention of the college boyfriend named Todd Merrill."

How right he was! Elissa grimaced wryly. "Todd got to California, saw all those blondes on the beach, and decided he didn't want a steady girlfriend."

"Pardon me if I state the obvious, but you're a blonde."

"Ah, but I didn't have a tan."

Gray laughed. Elissa couldn't help but smile, too. After the initial jolt to her ego, Todd Merrill's frenzied conversion to his idea of a West Coast playboy had been a source of amusement to her. He even wore gold chains and called everyone "babe."

"Why don't you go ahead and call your friend back now, Lissy?" Gray suggested. "I have to take Mandy home." He paused. "And by the way, you are going to that dance on Friday. Don't even think about not showing up, because I'll come after you and drag you there."

"You have the most charming way of asking a woman out. And to the most exciting places!" She gave him a limp smile, her voice saccharinely sweet. "Whatever could top the thrill of chaperoning the Halloween Fall Dance with you?"

"Good night, Elissa." Gray left, laughing.

Elissa, on the other hand, did not feel like laughing at all.

Ten

Only a few students wore Halloween costumes to the Fall Dance, though the cheerleaders, who sponsored the event, had tried to promote the idea of dressing up. However, it was common knowledge that the cheerleaders themselves refused to wear costumes, and this fact dealt a lethal blow to their promotion efforts.

Gray and Elissa chose to wear jeans and shirts—his favorite blue chambray and her white blouse with multicolored jewel-shaped buttons. They stood together by the punch bowl, guarding it against any student attempts to spike it with alcohol. Heavy-metal music blasted from the speakers at roaring volume while boys and girls drifted in and out of the gym, looking bored. Hardly anybody danced.

"Riverview's dances haven't changed a bit since I was in high school," Elissa said. She had to stand on tiptoe and practically shout into Gray's ear to be heard. "They're as awful as I remembered."

"It wasn't like this at our high school in Columbus," Gray said, leaning down. His mouth was too close to Elissa's ear, his lips were almost touching her skin. "We always had live bands who played great music and everybody danced every dance."

She steeled herself against the responsive shiver his nearness evoked. "It sounds like a scene from an Archie and Veronica comic book. And I don't believe you, anyway. All high school dances are like this. Hell on earth, especially for the unfortunate chaperones. Oh, I just hate this!"

What made it particularly hard to take, what was affecting her far worse than the terrible music and disaffected atmosphere, was having to stand around making impersonal small talk with Gray. Every conversation they'd had since the revelation of Gordon's death, earlier in the week, had been general, bland, and entirely superficial. Why, she'd had more personal exchanges with callers who'd dialed a wrong number! And she was well aware that there would be no meaningful talk of any kind that night, not in the raucous Riverview gym.

"I'd rather be home helping Aaron with his spelling," she muttered.

"Speak up, I can't hear you," Gray said. His jovial high spirits were in marked contrast to Elissa's. "You're going to have to borrow a megaphone and scream into my ear. Incredibly enough, somebody just pumped up the volume."

"And it's going to get pumped down right now!"

Fired with determination, Elissa headed toward the stage where the student disc jockey had just raised the decible-level to a dangerous, eardrum-rupturing high. She ordered him to turn it down, then down some more, until she could hear her own thoughts in her head instead of the unintelligible lyrics.

She returned to find Seth and his girlfriend, Brenda, standing by the punch bowl with Gray. "Jeez, Elissa, this is embarrassing," Seth complained. "It's bad enough you're here spying on us, but then you make Matt turn down the sound so low you can hardly hear it."

A blatant overexaggeration on his part, but one

Elissa wished were actually true. She made no reply but she did roll her eyes and look pointedly at her watch.

"I suggest you check a calendar instead," Gray said dryly. "We've been here at least three months."

"Are you two going to dance?" Brenda asked, staring interestedly from Gray to Elissa.

"This music isn't for dancing, Brenda, it's for head-banging," Gray said. "We'll pass on that, thanks."

"Would you dance if Matt played a slow song?" she persisted. She was a pretty hazel-eyed brunette, the first and only girl in Riverview to command fickle Seth Emory's interest for as long as six months. Her hold on him showed no sign of slackening, and Elissa wondered if Seth's and Gray's man-to-man talks concerned that particular hold.

"I'm going to tell Matt to play something we can dance to," Brenda decided, and flounced off, Seth following in her wake.

"Brenda doesn't ask, she orders," Gray said with amusement. "I see a bright future for her as a prison guard or a drill instructor at Marine boot camp. Not that she's in your league yet, but—"

"Are you implying that I'm domineering?" Elissa cut in, stung.

"Implying?" He grinned, his eyes gleaming.

He might have been teasing or flirting, or even both, but Elissa was too off balance to realize that and respond in kind. "I am not domineering," she said hotly. "I have strength and confidence, but I suppose that can be misinterpreted by those who find it threatening."

She walked away from him, feeling hurt. A moment later, a slow song, one with a recognizable tune and understandable lyrics that were not screamed or grunted, filled the cavernous gym.

Elissa watched Brenda take Seth's hand and pull him into the middle of the floor. Several other couples joined them, and by the end of the song many of the students were dancing together. They looked so young and sweet, she thought, an unexpected nostalgia sweeping over her.

"You didn't dance with Coach McCall, Elissa," Brenda said, coming over after the song was done.

"He didn't ask me, Brenda. Anyway, he can't leave his station. He's duty bound to protect the punch bowl."

Brenda frowned. "Are those rumors going around about you and him true? Seth and I don't know whether to believe them or not. Are you really Coach McCall's girlfriend?"

Another song began to play, Rod Stewart's cover of the old classic, "You Are Everything." Elissa braced herself against the sensual yearning evoked by the music and lyrics. Brenda gladly gave in to it. "I'm going to grab Seth and dance with him again," she said, her eyes dreamy.

"Seth is manning the punch bowl," Gray said behind them, startling them both. "Why don't you keep him company and make sure nothing happens to the punch while Elis—Miss Emory and I dance together, Brenda?"

Brenda's eyes widened. "So it is true!" She walked off to join Seth, looking pleased with her newfound knowledge.

"You realize," Elissa said coolly, "that if we step out onto that dance floor, we'll be confirming every rumor going around about us, from the G- to the X-rated ones. And leaving Seth in charge of the punch bowl is about as wise as trusting Mrs. Yoder's cats to fetch Peep from the oak tree. Seth and his friends tried to spike the punch at the prom last year and were given in-school suspension for three days."

"Which is why I also assigned the formidable Brenda to the task." Gray took Elissa's hand. "No one will dare mess with the punch while she's standing guard."

"Yes, we dragon ladies are a terrifying bunch.

Dominating, tenacious, ferocious." She pulled her hand away from his. "And no, I'm not going to dance with you. Why would you even want to talk to such a threatening she-devil, let alone dance with one?"

"Because I don't find you threatening."

"Oh, yes, you do!" She saw it clearly now. Little had changed since they'd met all over again as man and woman, updating their earlier roles of teacher and adoring schoolgirl. Gray would let her get only so close and then, invariably, he'd drop his impenetrable guard. The past week's shutout after their too-close, too-threatening talk about Gordon was the latest case in point. Being the tenacious, ferocious, domineering type, she had refused to give up. "And suddenly I'm very tired of it," she said, finishing her thoughts aloud.

Gray reacted immediately to her withdrawal. He snatched her hand back and yanked her onto the dance floor with him. "I know what you're doing. You're gearing up for a fight. But it's not going to happen."

Though she discreetly hissed a protest, he molded her against his hard, warm body and began a slow dance. "I don't want to fight with you, Elissa."

"You should have thought of that before you insulted me and hurt my feelings." Despite her best effort to remain stiff and tense in his arms, she found herself effortlessly following his lead, swaying rhythmically against him in time to the music.

"I was just kidding around, Lissy." He cupped the back of her head and gently pressed her cheek to his chest. His fingers threaded into her silky hair and he began to massage her scalp.

She tried hard to remain impervious to him. "Here we go again. One step forward, immediately followed by two backward. And just so you can't deliberately miss the point, let me clue you in. I'm not talking about dancing."

"Elissa, if I insulted you or hurt your feelings, I'm

sorry. I didn't intend to. I was joking, I wanted to make you laugh." His other hand moved slowly up and down her back.

"Ha! There, I laughed."

His lips twitched. "That's not exactly what I had in mind."

"You know, there's truth in jest, Gray." She fought the traitorous urge to close her eyes and melt against him. Her hungry body urgently wanted to. Already her breasts were swelling against his chest. Her nipples were tight and straining, and she felt a provocative urge to rub them against him.

Her eyelids dropped shut, but she instantly snapped them open. "And the truth is that you think I'm a dom—"

"—warm, beautiful, exciting woman who I want more than anything else in the world."

She drew back and stared into his eyes, which were burning with an intensity she knew well. She drew a quick breath. "You do?"

He scowled. "Don't playact, Elissa. You know very well how much I want you."

"I know that you used to want me," she said shakily. "But lately I haven't been too sure. Not sure at all."

His expression softened. "Why is that, baby?" He began to knead the sensitive hollow at the base of her spine.

Ribbons of heat flared through her. "You haven't touched me in weeks. We've spent hours together and you haven't even tried to kiss me. You keep me at arm's length, and I mean that both literally and figuratively."

"And you thought I wasn't attracted to you any-more?"

"I knew you never wanted to be in the first place. I was beginning to think you'd been successful in turning me into a friend or a sister instead of . . ."

"I guess if I were to call you a maddening little

idiot, you'd take offense and think I was insulting you again." His mouth was against her ear, his voice husky and seductive.

"I would definitely take offense," she murmured. He was hard and heavy and stirring against her, and she pressed even closer to him. "So don't do it."

"Then let me remind you that it was your idea to spend quality time together, without the distraction of sex. Being the gentleman that I am, I went along with you. Reluctantly to be sure, but I did accede to your wishes."

"You acceded to them extremely well," she said ruefully. "You adopted an unshakable hands off-policy when I only meant—"

"That was the only way I could handle it," he said. "When it comes to you, it's all-or-nothing for me, Elissa. And since you'd made it clear that all was out, it had to be nothing. I wanted you so badly, I couldn't trust myself to stop with just a few kisses. I couldn't keep turning it on and off. I feel like a matchhead striking flint every time I touch you, Elissa. On fire, burning up."

She swallowed. "That's the way it is for me, too, with you."

"I know. Which is another reason why I had to hold back. I knew I could get you into bed, but you'd asked me not to." He shook his head. "So there you have it. If I seduced you, you would resent me for it. If I put a lock on my raging lust, I'd keep your goodwill. What a choice! It hasn't been easy, Elissa."

She gazed up at him, her eyes shining. "No, it hasn't."

"Excuse me, Miss Emory and Coach McCall," sounded a clear young voice, cutting into their impassioned conversation.

It took Elissa and Gray a few moments to respond. They had been so completely absorbed in each other that their surroundings had faded into a muted inconsequential background, along with everybody in it. They could only stare dazedly at the bright-eyed cheerleader, Carolyn Conn, who seemed to have materialized magically before them.

But Carolyn was very real. "I'm sorry to interrupt," she said politely.

Gray and Elissa realized they were still holding each other and that the song was over. They swiftly parted and attempted to recapture the guard-dog mien of a proper high school dance chaperone.

"What is it, Carolyn?" Elissa asked, her eyes straying compulsively to Gray. He winked at her.

"I thought you'd want to know that somebody has poured two bottles of vodka into the water of the tub being used to bob for apples," Carolyn said.

"Oh, no!" Elissa frowned. "It better not have been my brother."

"It wasn't Seth," Carolyn assured her. "Brenda's watching him and the punch bowl. I can't tell you who spiked the apple tub because I don't want to squeal," she added earnestly.

"We understand, Carolyn," Gray said. "Thanks for your help."

The girl scurried off, and Elissa sighed. "Now we have to empty that tub."

Gray gave her a warning glance.

"Our discussion isn't over, Elissa."

She blushed. They had been interrupted at a crucial moment—Gray's revelation that he was so confident of her surrender, he knew he could take her to bed whenever he chose. It was not a theme she cared to dwell upon.

She directed her energies in another direction entirely. "I wonder if we can save the apples by washing them off? Miss Warburton said we were supposed to store any leftover apples in the cafeteria refrigerator so the cooks can make something with them on Monday."

"Now who's taking two steps backward after a big

one forward? And just so you can't deliberately miss the point, I'm not talking about dancing either."

"Gray, this isn't the time or the place," she whispered frantically. "Oh, good heavens, look over there! Justin Crothers just jumped into the tub of apples! And there goes Sam Wojik right in after him. They're lolling around like a pair of water buffaloes!"

"Ah, the stuff we chaperones live for," Gray said drolly. "Okay, intervention is definitely called for, but we're not through talking, Elissa. Not by a long shot. We've just straightened out one stupid misunderstanding between us, but at the rate we're going, we're going to get sandbagged again."

He started toward the group of students who were cheering on the boys' antics in the bathtub-sized metal tub. Elissa had to take three steps to his every one to keep up with him, but just before they reached the crowd he paused and turned to her.

"We've become good friends, Elissa." His voice was a smooth, seductive purr. "But it's not enough, not for either of us. Tonight we become lovers. And from now on, that's what we're going to be. Lovers *and* friends. Not one, not the other, but both."

For Elissa, the rest of the evening unfolded like a surrealistic dream. Physically she was present in the gym and she went through the motions of chaperoning, but the activity going on around her didn't seem quite real. Gray's words burned through her brain. *Tonight we become lovers.*

It wasn't going to happen, of course. Becoming lovers required privacy, and there was none of that to be had at the Emory house. But, oh, how she wished it were possible! Merely thinking about making love with Gray sent sensual shivers coursing through her. In a dreamy haze she relived every time he'd kissed her, every time he'd touched her, and the urgent needs of her own body surprised her. She was in love as she'd never been before, and making love with the man she loved promised to be a wondrous culmination of all her feelings, hopes, and dreams.

She felt nervous and excited and completely off balance, and she chided herself for giving free rein to her fantasies. She was going to have a difficult time calming down and cooling off that night in her own bed. For despite her penchant for daydreams, she was a realist, and there was nothing more real than the presence of her father and three younger brothers.

Gray viewed the situation differently. Applying his ingrained coaching principles, he had been focusing and concentrating on making love to Elissa since their whispered confessions while they were dancing. Now he was about to make it happen.

As the dance drew to an end, he dispatched Seth and Brenda to stay with Aaron and Andrew until their father returned from work after midnight. "You're spending the night with me," he told Elissa as he walked with her to the school parking lot. It was deserted, as they were the last to leave the building.

"I can't do that, Gray," she said wistfully.

"Yes, you can. You want to and you're going to."

"Gray, I know I'm twenty-five-years old, I know I've lived away from home during college and those three years in California, but my father has some very old-fashioned ideas. He still thinks of me as his little girl and he will have a conniption if he knows that I'm spending the night in a man's bed. Plus, I'm expected to set an example for my little brothers."

"Don't worry, honey, I've taken care of everything. I've had plenty of time to come up with a workable plan—all those hours that I've spent lying awake and alone in bed, wanting you beside me."

His gaze glided over her, studying her in the glow cast by the nearby street light. She was slim and femininely compact, her skin radiant and smooth, the features of her face distinct with character and strength as well as beauty. He knew he had never wanted any woman so badly, just as he knew that his feelings for her were so much more than a lusty physical attraction. Yes, he wanted her body; her mouth under his, her breasts in his hands, and her legs wrapped around him, her sweet, soft heat sheathing him. But he wanted more. He wanted all of her, her laughter and her love, her very essence.

A few weeks ago that realization would have unnerved him beyond measure and literally sent him running to blot out such alarming feelings. Perhaps he wouldn't have even been capable of acknowledging it, or the fact that these feelings flooding through him—this wild and urgent explosion of lust and tenderness, of anticipation and need—did not alarm him at all. He felt strong and vibrant and wonderfully, marvelously alive.

"So here's my plan." He smiled down at her. "I told Seth to tell your father that you're spending the night at your old pal Connie Ware's place."

"Pretending to spend the night at a girlfriend's?" Elissa uttered a groan mixed with a laugh. "That's the most unoriginal plan I've ever heard. I think it's been around since biblical times. Adam and Eve's daughter probably used it."

"I never said it was original. On the other hand, it's going to work. Remember when I went outside earlier this evening to chase the beer drinkers out of the bushes?"

She nodded.

"Well, after I did, I stopped at the pay phone and called Connie. I remembered her mentioning in the art room that she was available for whatever needed to be done. I wasn't sure what she was volunteering for, but I thought I'd take her up on her offer. She came through with flying colors. If your father or brothers should happen to call her place looking for you tonight, she's going to call you at my place immediately."

Elissa grimaced. "I feel as gauche and adolescent

as those beer drinkers you chased out of the bushes.
I'm sorry, Gray. We're two consenting adults, definitely of legal age, but . . ."

"I understand that you respect your father's feelings and that you're considering your impression-
able kid brothers, Elissa," Gray said quietly. "I respect
you for it." He opened the passenger door of the Jeep
Cherokee and half lifted her inside. "Come home
with me tonight, Elissa."

She laid her hands on his shoulders. Her heart
was pounding as she voiced the commitment she'd
made with her heart a long time ago. "I love you,
Gray."

They drove straight to his condo, and though the
sexual tension and anticipation was a tangible thing
between them, they talked and laughed with no
uneasiness or constraint between them. They were
comfortable with each other, one of the benefits of
the weeks they'd spent as friends.

When they entered his darkened living room,
though, their friendship sparked into passionate
flames. Gray picked Elissa up in his arms and
carried her to his bedroom. He set her on her feet
beside the bed, and they gazed at each other raptly,
hungrily.

"You're so beautiful," he said, stroking the sleek
line of her throat, then cupping her jaw to tilt her face
up to him. With leisurely sensuality he slanted his
head, fitting his mouth to hers to make the contact
deep, the pressure excitingly firm. His tongue entered her mouth and she welcomed it, pleasure
chasing through her body in an instant heady surge.

They kissed and kissed, and Elissa tightened her
arms around him, locking herself to him, as a mind-
less whimper of delight escaped from her throat. His
mouth was hot and demanding, and she loved it. She
loved him, and her body gloried in the sensations he
was arousing. She was aching for his touch, and
with every stroke of his hand, every deft caress of his
fingers, that ache intensified.

Gray unbuttoned her blouse and unclipped her bra, divested her of both, then lay down with her on the bed. He'd spent many fevered hours imagining this, how she would look, and now he knew. Her breasts were round and full, tipped with pink nipples that were taut with arousal.

"I've been wanting to see you, to taste you," he said raspily. He lowered his head to her breast and laved the tight pink buds with his tongue. When he drew one into his mouth, she cried out her arousal and her pleasure.

His hands glided to her waist and over her belly, followed the curves of her hips and the rounded firmness of her thighs. Elissa arched and moaned, and suddenly it was not enough to lie under his hands. She wanted to conduct a passionate exploration of her own, and pulled his shirt free from his jeans. Boldly she placed her hand against the fly of his jeans and stroked the hard male warmth within. He groaned with pleasure.

Neither could tolerate the barrier of their clothing for another second. Laughing at their own eagerness, they undressed each other, tossing away each discarded garment. One of Elissa's more inspired throws sent his shorts halfway across the room.

Naked at last, they lay together, their kisses becoming more frantic, their caresses hotter and bolder and devastatingly intimate. Gray pulled her down to him and she pressed against him, unable to get enough of him. His mouth was hungry, his hands demanding, but her own hunger and demands matched his, and their passion burned brighter, flared higher.

She clung to him, her legs splayed wide, her hands loving the strength of his muscles and the smoothness of his skin, marveling in the sensual contrast. Tension pounded through him and she sensed he was fighting for control, even as he seemed to be giving in to the wildfire between them.

"I want you so much, Gray," she said, speaking the

words she'd wanted to say for weeks. "I love you, I love you!"

Gray had no words, only feelings so strong and intense that he knew he was about to go under, caught in the swirling tide of need Elissa evoked within him. He managed to keep his wits long enough to reach into the drawer of the nightstand for that vital foil packet, then Elissa took over, driving him completely out of his head with her sexy, loving ministrations.

He surged into her, and her body adjusted and accommodated him as if she'd been made for him. As they moved together in sensual rhythm, the gliding pressure and heat building into an excitement so searing, a rapture so shattering, he began to believe that she *had* been made for him, just as he had been made for her. And now finally, finally, they were together.

Elissa clung to him, pulling him deeper into her, crying mindlessly as the flare of ecstasy consumed her. Gray immersed himself in her, losing himself to her as they became one, bonded together by the stunning pleasure that exploded within them. . . .

Eleven

They lay drowsy and sated in each other's arms in the cool, dark silence of the bedroom. Words seemed an unnecessary intrusion, so united were they in mind, body, and spirit. Gray watched Elissa's eyelids close as she drifted off to sleep. He tried to think some profound thoughts, but he was too physically and emotionally replete. He had given all, holding nothing back, and for the first time in years he felt free of that consuming, soul-haunting loneliness that had desolated his life.

The sharp ring of the telephone was as unexpected and jolting as the backfire of a truck. He jerked upright and rubbed his temples, feeling oddly dazed. Elissa, who'd been tossed onto the pillows like a ragdoll by his sudden leap forward, slowly raised herself on her elbows.

"It must be Connie," she said, groaning. Who else would be calling at the ungodly hour of—she glanced exhaustedly at the clock—three-eleven? She crawled over Gray and across the bed to reach the phone on the nightstand. He remained immobile, staring at the phone as if trying to guess its function.

A second later Elissa handed him the receiver. "It's

for you," she said, suddenly wide awake. A woman was on the line, and it wasn't Connie Ware.

"Jackie!" Gray exclaimed. Instantly he was alert and wide-eyed, tensely clutching the phone. "Jackie, what's wrong?"

Elissa's stomach clenched. Something couldn't have happened to Mandy! It would be too cruel, too terrible to be borne. Gray had suffered so many losses and he adored that child. She breathed a silent prayer.

"He left? He just walked out?" The panic left Gray's voice and was replaced by incredulous indignation. "He said he wanted *what*?"

Elissa listened, tension seeping through her. She tried to piece together what was happening from Gray's increasingly angry responses, but couldn't make much sense of it. Jackie was doing most of the talking, and crying. She knew that because Gray kept interjecting. "Jackie, honey, don't cry," when he wasn't muttering about "that jerk, that jackal, that lowlife Whittier!"

"I'll be right over, Jackie," he finally said. He hung up the phone and leaped out of bed, snapping on the bedside light. He began to gather his scattered clothes.

The sight of them brought back vivid memories of the passionate and frenetic removal of those clothes, and Elissa felt her cheeks grow warm in sensual reminiscence. As she watched Gray dress with the same speed that he had undressed just a few hours earlier, she was sure there was a grim irony in this somewhere. She was too rattled to appreciate the nuances of it, though.

"Gray, what's going on?" she asked. She felt a sinking sensation when he looked at her as if he were surprised to see her there. Had Jackie's late-night call obliterated her very existence from his mind?

"Paul and Jackie had a big fight and he walked out on her," Gray said. "He left her, all alone and crying."

"Does this happen often?" Elissa asked, trying to sound nonjudgmental. It was difficult, for she was beginning to form a very definite opinion of Jackie's middle-of-the-night phone call following her lover's quarrel with Paul.

"It's never happened before," Gray said tersely. "Poor Jackie is so upset, she's practically in hysterics. I have to go over there and calm her down."

"You have to drive the whole way to Blairsville at three o'clock in the morning because Jackie had a fight with Paul?" A terrible thought struck her. "Gray, did he—did Paul hit her?"

"Of course not! But tonight he broke the news that he's been offered a promotion that involves a move to Cincinnati. He wants to take the job and asked Jackie to move up the wedding date so she can move there with him." Gray was completely dressed now except for his shoes. He sat down to put them on.

Holding the sheet around her to preserve some shred of modesty, Elissa slid down the bed to sit beside him. She laid her hand on his shoulder. "Gray, that's not an unreasonable request for Paul to make. Since he and Jackie are going to be married, they—"

"They're not!" Gray exclaimed, standing up. When he did her hand was flung aside. "Paul unofficially told his boss that he'd accept the new job and Jackie was furious with him for expecting her to move. Then Paul lost his temper, too, and they had this big argument and now the engagement is off. Well, thank God for that!"

Elissa's eyes widened. "They broke up?" An ominous feeling set her stomach churning. "And you're glad?" She bit her lower lip so hard, she tasted blood. She tried not to give in to the terrible doubts assailing her. Maybe it wasn't as bad as she thought. She clung to that hope. "What about Mandy? How is she going to take this? She seems very fond of Paul."

"Mandy is just a child. And Paul worked very hard at winning her over."

"You make it sound like a crime," Elissa said uneasily. "I see nothing wrong and everything admirable about Mandy's potential stepfather trying to develop a positive relationship with her." The man had succeeded in his aims too. Elissa remembered how pleased the little girl had been while talking about living in the same house with her new daddy.

Then it hit her. Maybe Mandy's new daddy was fated to be the man who had been acting as her unofficial daddy all these years. Her late father's twin brother, her devoted uncle Gray.

But it wasn't only Mandy to whom Gray was devoted. Elissa went white. Gray had jumped from the bed he was sharing with her, on the very night they had consummated their love, to rush to Jackie's side. To celebrate the end of her engagement? To take advantage of the break to make his own move on his brother's lovely widow?

Elissa realized how little she knew of Jackie and Paul's relationship, its length and strength and depth. Gray had not discussed it with her, not even casually. He hadn't mentioned Paul Whittier until Mandy had innocently broken the news of his existence. Suddenly, it seemed odd and inauspicious that Gray had never acknowledged the other man in Jackie's life.

Because it was too painful for him to consider, let alone talk about? She was well aware of Gray's fantastic ability to block out what hurt, and she could easily picture him responding to Jackie's engagement to another man in the same way. Pretending that it hadn't happened, acting as if it hadn't.

Pain wrenched her, and she wanted to sob with the force of it. She watched in shock as Gray headed out the bedroom door without a single glance at her. "You're going to just walk away without even saying good-bye?" she cried out.

He stopped and ran his hand through his hair, looking upset and distracted. "I'm sorry. I just—It's such a—I have to go, but I'll call you."

The classic brush-off line. Elissa fought back tears. "Never mind," she said stiffly. "Don't bother."

"Why won't you understand? This is an emergency! Jackie needs me!" His voice rose as did his level of agitation.

"What Jackie needs is to sit down with Paul and talk to him, adult-to-adult."

Gray looked at Elissa but he didn't see her. The words she spoke didn't register in his head. Other words from another woman in another time were echoing in his head, and he was gripped by a chilling, shocking sense of déjà-vu. Memories of the pain his ex-wife had inflicted on him drove him to lash out at Elissa.

"You're behaving exactly like Lily!" he shouted. "She was jealous of anybody who had a claim on my time and affection, even my own brother. She resented every moment I spent away from her, she hated Gordon for being sick and Jackie and Mandy for needing me." His voice rose and then broke. "It was sheer hell, and dammit, no woman is going to put me through that hell again!"

He strode out of the room and out of the house. Elissa heard the front door slam shut, heard an engine roar as he drove off into the night. Drove off to console the weeping, vulnerable, beautiful Jackie, who might just be the love of his life.

And what does that make me? Elissa walked to the window and stared at the stars through her tears. Despair washed over her as she remembered the crucial omission that had occurred before, during, and after their passionate lovemaking. Gray hadn't once told her he loved her, though she had freely proclaimed her love for him.

She had never been one to hide from painful truths, but she wished she could escape from this one. Gray was the love of *her* life, yet it appeared she was just a footnote in his, a way for him to pass the time while Jackie was otherwise involved. Now Jackie was free and Gray couldn't even wait until the sun came up to hotfoot it to her side. And into her bed?

"I don't know what to say, Elissa." Connie was uncharacteristically subdued as she and Elissa sat at her kitchen table sipping hot tea. Elissa had called her friend a half hour ago to pick her up at Gray's place, and Connie had loyally done so despite the hour, bringing Elissa to her apartment, no questions asked. Elissa needed to talk, though, and had shared parts of her sad tale.

"When Gray called me earlier," Connie said, "to ask if I'd cover for you tonight, he seemed so upbeat, so happy. He sounded like a man madly in love, Lissy. I was sure you and Gray were meant for each other."

Once again, Elissa blinked back the tears that had been threatening since Gray's abrupt departure. "I'm not going to sit around feeling sorry for myself," she vowed fiercely. "Don't indulge me, Connie. Give me a pep talk, give me a lecture, tell me to cheer up because—"

"—this is actually the luckiest thing that could've happened to you," Connie finished for her, reciting one of the universal lines used to buoy spirits and soothe hurts. "Okay, give me a little time to come up with some more of the old stock phrases." She sighed. "It's better to have loved and lost than never loved at all. There're plenty of other fish in the sea. You're going to make some lucky guy a terrific wife. You deserve someone better. Smile, it's not the end of the world." She paused. "How am I doing? How are *you* doing?"

Elissa managed a tremulous smile. "I feel better

already." She swallowed the lump that seemed to have lodged permanently in her throat. "But I'm really tired. I think I'll go to bed now." She gave her friend a swift, heartfelt hug. "Connie, thanks for everything. I don't know what I would have done without you tonight."

She borrowed a pair of Connie's pajamas—dark green shorts and a matching shirt that looked more like sportswear than sleepwear—and slipped beneath the covers of the day bed in the small crowded den. Shivering and alone in the darkness, she felt the tears she'd been keeping at bay begin to stream down her cheeks.

"I'll get over this," she told herself over and over, whispering the words like a litany. First, she thought, she must focus and concentrate on something, anything other than Gray McCall and how much she loved him. Think of next week's art projects, plan the menus for the mouth of November. Picture the family intact and reunited with Mom back to her energetic, competent self. Imagine herself getting on a plane to return to California, the sun and the beach.

The visual images weren't working. With every one came another of Gray. She saw him smiling, frowning, laughing, grimacing, teasing, leaning over her, his dark eyes intense as he thrust into her. . . .

Elissa sat up. The silence was becoming oppressive. She needed sound, and quickly located Connie's Walkman, which she'd seen earlier on the small table near the window. Connie's tastes ran to alternative music, and Elissa slipped a tape into the small machine and slipped the headphones over her ears. After a few moments of listening, she wished for an alternative to the alternative music, but even it was better than the lonely, dark silence. She could hear nothing but the oddly discordant melody, and she lay back down and closed her eyes.

Two songs later the door swung open and she sat

up, blinking at the shaft of light streaming in from the hallway. Her heart began to pound. Was she dreaming? Or having hallucinations? Standing in the doorway was Gray himself, wearing the jeans and blue chambray shirt she'd seen him throw on approximately one hour and fifteen minutes ago.

But no, neither her eyes nor her mind were playing tricks on her. Behind Gray stood Connie, wrapped in a paisley-silk robe, her eyes glowing with excitement. Elissa whipped off the headset. "Connie, how could you?" She did not look at either Connie or Gray, and her voice was as cold as winter ice. "I thought you understood that I—"

"Elissa, will you marry me?" Gray asked.

"Now do you see why I let him in?" Connie exclaimed eagerly. "I heard him pounding at the front door, and when I saw it was him, I told him to beat it. But he said he wanted to ask you to marry him. I couldn't turn away a prospective marriage proposal, Elissa! He's what you've been wanting since you were seventeen years old!"

Elissa flushed scarlet. Discretion had never been one of Connie's strong points. "You're wrong, Connie. I do not want to marry a man who's in love with another woman."

"But he's not!" Connie cried. "Why would he propose to you if he loved—"

"Connie, would you excuse us, please?" Gray said. "I appreciate your support, but I can speak for myself, thanks."

Connie shrugged. "I'm going to order a pizza. Maybe by the time it's delivered, you'll have straightened this whole mess out." She left the room, carefully closing the door behind her.

"Go away, Gray," Elissa said wearily, turning away from him.

"No." He crossed the small room in three strides and knelt down beside the bed. "I'll never leave you again, Elissa. I love you. I want to spend the rest of my life proving to you how much."

She didn't look at him. "May I assume from your sudden change of heart that Jackie and Paul have patched things up and you're back in the market for a cook and a bedroom companion?"

He rose to sit on the edge of the narrow bed. She moved as far away from him as she could, which unfortunately wasn't far enough. "I hurt you," he said, and his voice was thick with regret. "I'm sorry, Elissa. I'm so sorry. If I could take back everything I said, if I could change the foolish, heartless way I acted, I would. Sweetheart, I wish I could."

"I'm nothing like your ex-wife," she said tightly. She felt her lower lip quiver and bit it, striving for control.

"I know, my love, I know. You're the warmest, sweetest, most loving and generous woman I've ever known. Not to mention the sexiest, the funniest . . . the list is endless, Elissa."

She folded her arms. "Why, Gray? What made you change your mind? Ninety minutes ago you couldn't get away from me fast enough. You thought I would make your life sheer hell. Now you claim I'm the most wonderful woman in the world and you want to marry me? I feel like a human yo-yo. I don't know what to think or believe, Gray."

Gray took both of her hands in his. They were icy cold, and he rubbed her palms to warm them. "I know I behaved like a raving lunatic and I don't blame you for doubting me, Elissa. What you have to know is . . ." He paused and grasped her chin between his thumb and his forefinger, turning her face to his. "I spent the last eight years on call for Jackie and Mandy, but this is the first time since Gordon's death that I've heard Jackie so upset, so distraught. I heard the pain and the panic in her voice and I freaked. She was alone and crying, just like before, and it was as if she were calling me to tell me that Gordon had taken a turn for the worse. I just clicked into that mode and I had to get there right away."

"And I got cast in the Lily role because I tried to get in your way," she said grimly. "Gray, nobody understands family ties and obligations more than I do. I would never stand between you and your family when they need you."

"I know you wouldn't, Elissa. By the time I arrived at Jackie's house, I'd managed to remember that I knew it."

"You didn't belong in the middle of Jackie and Paul's argument," she added. "That's called interference, Gray, and it's very different from being supportive."

He rested his elbows on his knees and held his head in his hand. "Sweetheart, believe me, I know that now too. As I was pulling into Jackie's driveway, I also knew I'd made a terrible, unforgivable mistake by going there, that I'd hurt you, the only woman I've ever really loved. I was turning the car around to come back when Jackie came outside. I was as upset as she was at that point, maybe even more so because she'd calmed down by then and was willing to concede that she'd overreacted to Paul's news."

"So Jackie and Paul are back together," Elissa said, staring intently at him. "Aren't you upset about that? You thanked God they'd broken up earlier."

He met her gaze. "I was shaken at the thought of Mandy moving to Cincinnati, and I hated Whittier's guts for walking out on Jackie when she was so upset." His face was a mask of pure chagrin. "All at once it occurred to me that I was guilty of the same sin, leaving *you* when you were upset. I felt like the jerk, jackal, lowlife that I'd accused Paul of being. And he's not that at all, Elissa. He genuinely loves Jackie and Mandy. The poor guy knocked himself out to get that promotion. It's a big salary increase and he wanted it for Jackie and Mandy, for the family they hope to have."

He shook his head ruefully. "Jackie and I sat around cursing ourselves for being the idiots we are. Then I suggested she call Paul to apologize and ask him to forgive her. He was on his way over when I left. I took my own advice, and here I am. I came over here before I went back to my place. I knew you wouldn't be there and I couldn't face being there without you. Will you accept my apologies and forgive me, Elissa?" He lifted her hands to his mouth and kissed every fingertip. "Darling, please?"

"Yes," she said flatly. "But you didn't have to propose for me to forgive you."

"I wanted to propose. I want to marry you, Elissa. You're not going back to California. You're going to stay here in Riverview with me and we're going to have smart, healthy kids who'll drive us nuts and we'll—"

"The pizza's here!" Connie sang out from the other room. "Are you two friends again yet?"

"I want to live with you," Gray continued urgently. "Legally, as soon as possible. If we don't get married right away, we'll have to keep inventing excuses to get you out of the house, and Connie will become an integral part of our relationship because we'll need her as an alibi and—"

"Stop!" She placed her fingers on his lips and smiled for the first time since he'd entered the room. It was a typical Elissa smile, lighting her whole face and lighting up his world.

"You don't have to resort to threats. I want to be with you, Gray. I love you." She slid closer, laying her hands on his chest, and her expression sobered. "That's why I was devastated when I thought you were only using me to take your mind off Jackie. That's why I was so hurt when I thought I'd lost you."

He enfolded her in his arms, and a great shudder of relief shook his body. "Ah, Elissa, that's not how it is. I love you and tonight I finally realized how much. You're part of everything I do and you're everything I want. With you I've found a happiness I never thought I would know or have. Tell me you'll always love me." His eyes misted. "And that you'll never let me go."

She gazed up at him, her own eyes brimming with tears. Tears of joy and a deep understanding and abiding love. "I love you and I always will," she whispered. She grinned suddenly. "And don't even think I'll let you get away from me. It took me eight years to *land* you and now, my darling trophy, you're all mine."

"Sounds like that makes you an honor graduate of the Connie Ware Man-Hunting School," he said dryly. "But I'm not complaining. You may not realize it yet, but you've been caught yourself. By me, the man who intends to love you more and more every day for the rest of our lives."

They kissed deeply, intimately, a kiss of passion and commitment, of a love that would never end.

"Let's go to my place," Gray said huskily, standing up with her in his arms. "I want to make love to you again, then make plans to get married as soon as possible."

"I still have to look after Daddy and the boys till Mom gets home. And she'll probably need my help around the house for a while afterward."

"I know. I don't mind spending afternoons and evenings there, and I don't mind heading down there in the mornings before school if necessary. But I want to be able to take my wife home at night. To spend all night, every night with you, holding you and loving you—"

"Okay, you two, that's enough!" Connie called. "Time to come out and help me eat this pizza!"

"—without having to depend on Connie to cover for us," he finished.

Elissa draped her arms around his neck. "Coach McCall, the answer is yes. Absolutely and unequivocally yes, yes, yes! Now, let's go and celebrate our engagement with a slice of pizza."

They left the little room holding hands, to begin their life together, a life destined to be long and happy and filled with much laughter and love.

THE EDITOR'S CORNER

There are certain stories we all know and love, whether they're fairy tales, classic novels, or unforgettable plays. We treasure them for the way they touch our heart and soul, make us laugh or cry—or both—and next month LOVESWEPT presents you with a bounty of **TREASURED TALES**, six wonderful romances inspired by beloved stories. With special messages from the authors and gorgeous covers featuring black-and-white photographs that reflect the timelessness of these stories, **TREASURED TALES** are worth a king's ransom!

Starting the lineup is Helen Mittermeyer with **'TWAS THE NIGHT**, LOVESWEPT #588, a stirring version of **BEAUTY AND THE BEAST**. It was on Christmas Eve that Rafe Brockman and Cassie Nordstrom first met, but then they parted as enemies. Now, years later, fate brings them together again on Christmas Eve, and they learn that the gift of love is the true Christmas miracle. A heartwarming story from one of the genre's most popular authors.

In **THE PRINCESS AND THE PEA**, LOVESWEPT #589, Fayrene Preston gives her heroine something more intriguing—and gorgeous—to deal with than a troublesome legume. Though Cameron Tate is the perfect hunk to star in a jeans commercial, all Melisande Lanier wants from him is his bed. But Cameron will sell only if workaholic Mel slows down long enough to fall in love with him. Fayrene's winning charm makes this enchanting story shine.

Like Sydney Carton in Charles Dickens's *A Tale of Two Cities,* Nick Atwell is a rebel with a taste for trouble, but his **RENEGADE WAYS**, LOVESWEPT #590 by Terry

Lawrence, can't dissuade Connie Hennessy from believing the handsome diplomat might be just the hero she needs. And she quickly lets Nick know she's willing to barter heated kisses for Nick's help in a perilous mission. Terry really lets the sparks fly between these two characters.

With **NIGHT DREAMS**, LOVESWEPT #591, Sandra Chastain gives us a hero as unforgettable as the Phantom from *The Phantom of the Opera*. No one knows the truth behind the legend of Jonathan Dream, the playboy who'd vanished after building an empire. But when Shannon Summers is taken to his castle to help his disabled daughter, she learns of his scars and his secrets—and burns with the wildfire of his desire. Sandra tells this story with stunning force.

Snow White was contented living with the seven dwarfs, but in **THE FAIREST OF THEM ALL** by Leanne Banks, LOVESWEPT #592, Carly Pendleton would like nothing better than for her seven loving, but overbearing brothers to let her have her own life. Longtime friend Russ Bradford agrees, especially since he has plans to claim her for his own and to taste the sweetness of her ruby-red lips. Leanne delivers a wonderfully entertaining read.

Peggy Webb will light up your day with **DARK FIRE**, LOVESWEPT #593. Although Sid Granger isn't as short on looks as Cyrano de Bergerac, he doesn't dare court the beautiful Rose Anne Jones because he thinks he can never match her perfection. Instead he agrees to woo her for a friend, but the thought of her in another man's arms sends the fighter pilot soaring to her side. Peggy has once again created an irresistible, sensuous romance.

On sale this month are four fabulous FANFARE titles. From *New York Times* bestselling author Amanda Quick comes **RECKLESS,** a tale of a tarnished knight, a daring maiden, and a sweet, searing, storybook love. When

Phoebe Layton needs help to carry out a quest, she can imagine no one more suited to the job than Gabriel Banner. But the Earl of Wylde has a quest of his own in mind: to possess Phoebe, heart and soul.

The Delaneys are here with **THE DELANEY CHRISTMAS CAROL!** For this long-awaited addition to this enduring family's saga, Kay Hooper, Iris Johansen, and Fayrene Preston teamed up once again, and now we're thrilled to give you three tales of three generations of Delaneys in love and of the changing face of Christmas— past, present, and future. Enjoy our special holiday offer to you.

If you missed Tami Hoag's novel **SARAH'S SIN** the first time around, you can pick up a copy now and discover a warm, moving story of two cultures in conflict and two hearts in love. Matt Thorne is every fantasy Sarah Troyer has ever had. And though there's a high price to pay for giving herself to one outside the Amish ways, Sarah dares to allow herself a brief, secret adventure in the arms of a forbidden man.

Maureen Reynolds has been described by *Romantic Times* as "a very HOT writer," and the tempestuous historical romance **SMOKE EYES** will show you why. Katherine Flynn has worked hard to overcome the double prejudice she faced as a woman and an Arapaho half-breed, but she can't win against the power of desire when Zach Fletcher abruptly returns to her life.

Also on sale this month in the Doubleday hardcover edition is **CONFIDENCES** by Penny Hayden. In the tradition of Danielle Steel, **CONFIDENCES** is a deeply moving novel about four "thirty-something" mothers and a long-held secret that could save the life of a seventeen-year-old boy.

Well, folks, it's around that time of year when people usually take stock of what they've accomplished and look forward to what's ahead. And one of the things we've been taking stock of is **THE EDITOR'S CORNER**. It's been a continuing feature in LOVESWEPT books since LOVESWEPT #1 was published. That makes almost ten years' worth of previews, and we wonder if it's still something you look forward to every month, or if there's something else you'd like to see perhaps. Let us know; we'd love to hear your opinions and/or suggestions.

Happy reading!

With warmest wishes,

Nita Taublib
Associate Publisher
LOVESWEPT and FANFARE

Don't miss these fabulous Bantam Fanfare
titles on sale in NOVEMBER.

RECKLESS
by Amanda Quick

THE DELANEY CHRISTMAS CAROL
by Kay Hooper, Iris Johansen,
and Fayrene Preston

SARAH'S SIN
by Tami Hoag

SMOKE EYES
by Maureen Reynolds

In hardcover from Doubleday,
CONFIDENCES
by Penny Hayden

In the bestselling tradition of Danielle Steel, CONFIDENCES
is a warm, deeply moving novel about four "thirty–something"
mothers, whose lives are interwoven by a long–held secret—a
secret that could now save the life of a seventeen-year-old boy
dying of leukemia.

RECKLESS
by Amanda Quick
the *New York Times* bestselling author of
RAVISHED and SCANDAL

From a crumbling fairy–tale castle on the stormy Sussex coast to a dazzling, dizzying masquerade ball comes an enchanting tale of a tarnished knight, a daring maiden, and a sweet, searing, storybook love. . . .

At sixteen Phoebe Layton had imagined that Gabriel Banner was a brave and valiant knight, a noble–hearted hero born to rescue ladies in distress. Which was why, eight years later, when she desperately needed help to carry out a vital quest, she could think of no one more suited to the job than Gabriel.

But when she lures her shining knight to a lonely midnight rendezvous, Phoebe finds herself sparring with a danger-ously desirable man who is nothing like the hero of her dreams, and when he sweeps her into a torrid—and bla-tantly unchivalrous—embrace, she can't help but fear that she's made a dreadful mistake. It's a kiss that will seal Phoebe's fate. For now the exciting Earl of Wylde has a quest of his own: to possess the most intriguing, impulsive, outrageous female he has ever met . . . even if he has to slay a dragon to do it.

THE DELANEY CHRISTMAS CAROL

by Kay Hooper, Iris Johansen, and Fayrene Preston

The Delaney Dynasty continues with three tales of Christmas—Past, Present, and Future

CHRISTMAS PAST

by Iris Johansen

From the moment he first laid eyes on her, Kevin Delaney felt a curious attraction for the rag–clad Gypsy beauty rummaging through the attic of his ranch at Killara. He didn't believe for a moment her talk of magic mirrors and second sight, but something about Zara St. Cloud stirred his blood. Now, as Christmas draws near, a touch leads to a kiss and a gift of burning passion as the Gypsy and the cowboy discover the sensual magic a man and a woman can make in each other's arms.

CHRISTMAS PRESENT

by Fayrene Preston

Bria Delaney had been looking for Christmas ornaments in her mother's attic when she saw him in the mirror for the first time—a stunningly handsome man with sky–blue eyes and red–gold hair. She had almost convinced herself he was only a dream when Kells Braxton arrived at Killara. Bria saw romance in their future as her mirror fogged with steamy kisses and late–night caresses. Soon shadow would turn to flesh and dreams to real–life passion as the rugged Australian stepped from her looking glass to lead them both to a holiday wonderland of sensuous pleasure.

CHRISTMAS FUTURE
by Kay Hooper

As the last of the Delaney men, Brett returned to Killara this Christmastime only to find it in the capable hands of his father's young and beautiful widow. Yet the closer he got to Cassie, the more Brett realized that the embers of their old love still burned and that all it would take was a look, a kiss, a caress to turn their dormant passion into an inferno. Could their love for each other redeem the past—and save Killara for a new generation of Delaneys?

The three endearing stories of The Delaney Christmas Carol *are unified by a magical mirror. The following excerpt from the book's foreword gives us a glimpse into the history of that enchanting glass.*

Like many stories surrounding the Delaney family, the truth of the mirror was somewhat clouded by conflicting tales. That wasn't unusual, particularly given Shamus Delaney's habit of freely embellishing his family's history, but it did sometimes cause problems for succeeding generations.

Even the most likely explanation for how the Delaney family came to have the mirror was vague, yet colorful. Stripped of all but the barest bones of the story, however, it seems that in his youth in Ireland, Shamus performed some service—about which he was uncharacteristically silent, even in his private journal—for a mysterious tribe of Gypsies. In return, a Gypsy artisan carved a lovely and elaborate frame from bogwood for an oval mirror of exceptional clarity.

Was the frame so special, or the mirror itself? In all the years afterward, no one was prepared to guess. Nor would any Delaney have dared to separate the dark bogwood from the brilliant perfection of the mirror in order to know for sure. For most, that question hardly mattered, because the undeniable fact was that the mirror was far more than glass and wood.

It was a window that offered brief glimpses into the past, present, and future of the Delaney family. But it was a capricious thing. The mirror revealed tragedy as often as triumph and refused to be mastered even by the willful Delaneys. Only some Delaneys saw anything other than their own reflections, and few indeed saw what they wanted to see even when the mirror opened its window into time.

Many of his descendants were divided on whether Shamus knew the true nature of the Gypsies' gift. Some said that he accepted the mirror and stumbled on the truth later, while others were certain that the Gypsies themselves had explained in language fanciful enough to satisfy even the most romantic the true nature of their gift when it was given.

Whatever actually happened during that presentation, time revealed the truth of the mirror. And no doubt there were many Delaneys in the years that followed who believed it was a window best left shuttered, because it wasn't wise for mortal eyes to gaze into the future.

Still, not even the Delaneys who might have wanted to, dared to destroy the mirror. They might well put it away, but it became as much a part of Delaney heritage as the bogwood clock. However, as things put out of sight sometimes fade out of mind, the mirror was either deliberately or accidentally forgotten by the family at various times through the years. Tucked away in an attic or shoved back into a dark corner, it waited patiently to be discovered or rediscovered.

Bits of its history were lost, for a time or forever. Whole generations of the family lived without knowing anything at all about the mirror. But then a curious explorer would find it again and become intrigued. It would be dusted off and polished and brought forth to be exclaimed over.

It possessed its own sense of timing. It always seemed to reappear in the family at critical moments. And, oddly, it favored holidays, particularly Christmas—perhaps because of the holly carved so intricately into its frame, or perhaps simply because Christmas was innately a magical time. In any case, the holiday seemed a perfect time to hang so lovely a thing in a room or hallway of Killara.

And who could resist a glance into a mirror of such exceptional clarity? Few. Most saw only their own reflection, but some saw more.

SARAH'S SIN
by Tami Hoag

"A master of the genre."
—*Publisher's Weekly*

From Tami Hoag, award-winning author of *Lucky's Lady* and *Still Waters*, comes ONE OF HER MOST BELOVED ROMANCES—a warm, moving story of two cultures in conflict and two hearts in love.

Matt Thorne had come to his sister's rural inn to recover from an injury, far from the city and his fast-paced life as an emergency room physician. Drifting between sleep and wakefulness, Matt didn't trust his eyes when he saw the young woman who sat at his bedside in her plain cotton dress and apron, her chestnut hair tucked demurely beneath a white bonnet, like a beautiful vision from the past century.

Sarah Troyer had been warned about the womanizing Dr. Thorne, but nothing prepared her for the shiver of desire that shook her to her core when she gazed at him. Though her life was bound by the simple Amish way, Sarah had always longed for the world outside. Sarah was willing to allow herself a brief, secret adventure in the arms of a forbidden man. But she hadn't counted on Matt's passionate love—a love that would not let go, a love that could cost them both everything they knew. . . .

"You are to stay in bed."

"My favorite place to be—provided I'm not alone."

"Well, you're sure going to be alone here," she said tartly, finding a little bit of the sass that had always bought her a glower of disapproval from her father. With this man it only seemed to generate more of his teasing humor.

He chuckled weakly, wincing a bit and laying a hand gingerly against the white bandage that swathed his ribs. "Oh, come on, Sarah. Have pity on a poor cripple. You're not really going to make me stay in bed all alone, are you?"

"You bet." She nodded resolutely.

"Then I'm afraid I'm going to have to make a speedy recovery. I can't stand the idea of having a beautiful nurse and not being able to chase her around the bed."

Beautiful. Sarah did her best to ignore his compliment. To accept a compliment was to accept credit for God's doing. It was *Hochmut*—pride—a sin. She didn't need to be charged with any more of them than she already had. So she brushed aside the warm glow that threatened to blossom inside her and decided to match him teasing for teasing. "The shape you're in, I'll have no trouble getting away."

Matt gave her a look. "Gee, don't spare my feelings here, Sarah. Lay it on the line."

"I'm sorry," she said, having the grace to blush. "I'm much too forthright. It's always getting me into trouble."

"Really?" Matt chuckled. "I can't imagine you in trouble."

"Ach, me, I'm in trouble all the time," she admitted, rolling her eyes. A secretive little Mona Lisa smile teased her lips as she stepped closer to the bed.

A sweet, warm feeling flooded through Matt. It wasn't exactly lust. It was . . . liking. Sarah Troyer was beguiling him with her innocence, and he would have bet she didn't have the vaguest idea she was doing it. "What kinds of things get you in trouble?"

Her smile faded and she glanced away. *Wishing for things I shouldn't want. Wanting things I can't have.* But her thoughts remained unspoken. The flush that stained her cheeks with color now was from guilt. She was what she was, and she should be grateful for the things she had, she reminded herself, tamping down the longing that sprang eternal in her soul. Like weeds in a garden, her father would say, they must be torn out by the roots. Somehow, she had never had the heart to dig that deep and tear out all her dreams.

She realized with a start that Matt was watching her, waiting for an answer. "Neglecting my work gets me into trouble," she said quietly, eyes downcast to keep him from seeing any other answers that might be revealed by those too-honest mirrors of her true feelings. "I had best go down and see to making you some supper."

"In a minute," Matt murmured, catching her by the wrist as she turned to go. Her skin was soft and cool beneath his fingertips, like the finest silk. He'd always had an especially acute sense of touch, and now he picked up the delicate beating of Sarah's pulse as if it were pounding like a jackhammer. He wondered if she would even know what a jackhammer was, and he marveled again at how untouched she seemed to him. He felt like the most jaded cynic in comparison.

She would know nothing about the kind of violence that had disrupted his life. Street gangs and drug wars and inner-city desperation were the trappings of another world, a world far removed from farm life and people who disdained automobiles as being too worldly.

He wanted to ask Sarah about the shadows that had crossed her face an instant before she had answered his question. He found he wanted to know all about her. He wrote it off as a combination of boredom and natural curiosity, and conveniently ignored the fact that he was not usually so curious about the deep, dark secrets of the women in his life.

It wasn't that he was so self-absorbed, he didn't care. It was more a matter of practicality. His career took precedence over all else in his life, and it left little time or energy for deep relationships. He wore his title of hospital Romeo with ease and good humor, and thought of all-consuming romantic love in only the most abstract of ways. So when Sarah Troyer turned back toward him, her eyes as blue as twin lakes under the sun and as round as quarters, he put the jolt in his chest down to a reawakening libido and counted himself lucky to be among the living.

"I think I might need a little help getting up," he said, his voice a notch huskier than usual.

"I think you might need to get your hearing checked," Sarah said breathlessly. She extricated her arm from his hold and stepped out of his reach, absently rubbing her wrist as if she could erase the tingling his touch had roused. "You are not to get out of bed."

"Fine," Matt said, scowling. "Don't help me. I'll manage."

Taking great care to move slowly, he eased his legs over the edge of the bed and waited for his head to stop swimming. Out of deference to Sarah's undoubtedly delicate sensibilities, he pulled the black-and-purple quilt around himself toga-style, then he took as deep a breath as his taped ribs would allow and rose.

The earth tilted drunkenly beneath his feet and he staggered forward in an effort to keep himself from falling. The quilt dropped away as he reached out to grab onto something—anything—to steady himself. The "something" his hands settled on gasped and squirmed. His eyes locked on Sarah's for an instant, an instant full of shock, surprise, and the unmistakable sparks of attraction, then they both went down in a tangle of arms and legs, quilt, and ankle-length cotton skirt.

Sarah gave a squeal as she landed on her back. Matt groaned as he came down on top of her, pain digging into his ribs and pounding through his head. A red-hot arrow of it shot down his left leg and a blissful blackness began to descend over him, beckoning him toward the peace of unconsciousness, but he fought it off. He sucked a breath in through his teeth, held it, expelled it slowly, all the while willing himself to remain in the land of the living.

After a moment that seemed like an eternity, the pain

receded. He slowly became aware of the feminine form cushioning his body. There really was a woman under all those clothes, he thought, mentally taking inventory of full breasts and shapely legs. His hands had settled at the curve of her waist, and he let his fingers trace the angles of it. She was trim but womanly. Very womanly, he thought, groaning again, but this time in appreciation as she shifted beneath him, and the points of her nipples grazed his chest through the cotton of her gown.

"Are you all right?" Sarah asked, trying to sound concerned as a whole array of other feelings assaulted her—panic, desire, guilt. Matt Thorne was pressed against the whole length of her, and while there might have been some question about his health, there was certainly no question about his gender. She squirmed frantically beneath him, only managing to come into even more intimate contact with him. She had automatically grabbed him as they had fallen, and now she found her hands gripping the powerful muscles of his upper arms. His skin was smooth and hot to the touch, and her fingers itched to explore more of it. How she managed to push the thought from her head and speak was beyond her. "Are you injured?"

"Me?" Matt said dreamily, his thick lashes drifting down as his smile curved his mouth upward. "I'm in heaven."

SMOKE EYES
by Maureen Reynolds

"a very HOT writer. . . . guaranteed to take
readers to new heights of sensuality."
—*Romantic Times*

*He was a dark–eyed captain home from the wild
sea . . . she was the exquisite treasure he had come
to plunder. . . .*

*With her gray eyes flashing fire, Katherine Flynn was torn between
anger and breathless awe at the sight of her old childhood friend. A
respected and dedicated doctor in a small Colorado town, she'd
worked hard to overcome the double prejudice she faced as a woman
and an Arapaho half–breed. Why had Zach come back after all these
years? Still one look at the dangerous, steel-muscled man he'd become
was enough to set her body burning with forbidden desire—and to
persuade her to risk everything for one stolen moment in a handsome
brigand's arms.*

In the following scene, Katherine is fetched by a deputy to come
to the jail to attend to an injured prisoner. . . .

Everyone who had been in the store followed Katherine
and Tom to the jail, jabbering excitedly up the front steps
and clumping behind them. When Katherine entered the
jail, she gasped at the sight of the sheriff with his gun trained
on the prisoner in the first cell. She did not even let her gaze
slide toward the prisoner, keeping it fixed on the gun instead.

"Good Lord, Sheriff!" she said. "Is that necessary?"

"He's dangerous, Doc. An animal! Lookit what he did to Tom there."

"He can't hurt you behind bars," Katherine said. Though she had not yet looked at the prisoner, she could feel his presence, big and dark and menacing. She sensed his gaze on her, and felt a waiting stillness in the air, as if they'd caged a tiger that was getting ready to pounce.

"Sheriff," she said, "let me into the cell so I can see if he needs suturing."

The sheriff jerked the pistol toward the keys hanging on the wall behind the desk, and Tom went to fetch them.

"You so much as *look* at her crossways," the sheriff warned the prisoner, "an' I'll blow yer head clear off."

The sheriff pulled back the trigger, and Katherine heard the sharp click of a cartridge. The prisoner made a low sound in his throat, and she turned to him in time to see him whirl around and stare out the small barred window at the rear of the cell. He was tall and lean with incredibly wide shoulders packed with iron muscle. Even beneath the fabric of his rough striped shirt she could see those hard muscles shift and ripple. Awed by the size of him, she let her gaze drift over his broad back, down to his lean waist, and lower, to where his black trousers clung to his form so intimately she could see the slight hollows in his tight, hard buttocks. A strange sensation flickered through her, and she quickly looked up at his rock-hard profile.

Tom unlocked the door and, with the sheriff muttering something behind her, Katherine stepped into the cell. The prisoner ignored her.

"Sir," she said, "would you please come sit on the bunk so I can tend to you?"

Slowly, he turned to face her. Because the light was behind him, she could not make out his features, but there was no denying his mocking tone. "Sir?" he repeated. "Have you forgotten, madam, that I am in this cell because I've been accused of murder?"

Katherine turned briskly to set her bag on the bunk and open it. She heard his booted heels strike the stone floor— once, twice—then he was beside her, and she could smell him, earthy and male.

With trembling fingers she rummaged through her bag while the big stranger settled himself on the bunk, long legs sprawled wide. After removing her coat, she laid her instruments on a rickety chair. When she turned to the prisoner, her heart stopped. Somehow she had ended up standing between his wide-spread legs.

She glanced at his face, still shadowed in the poorly lit cell. Quickly she averted her eyes to the opened skin under a lock of thick black hair, matted with blood. As she moved closer to him she could almost feel his amused gaze on her face. She ignored it and pushed his hair aside to reveal the wound near his temple, still trickling blood. "You'll need a stitch or two," she said.

He didn't answer, but she was aware that he watched her face with a quiet intensity. She kept her own eyes lowered as she swiftly threaded a needle with a length of catgut. Stepping close again, she lifted the needle and told him to keep still. He didn't flinch as the needle pierced his skin, but he did speak.

"Are you going to tell that inept excuse for a lawman to take his gun off my head, Smoke Eyes?"

Katherine jolted as if someone had put a cattle prod to her flesh. The needle dropped from her nerveless fingers as she stared at the man as if she'd seen a ghost. And she may as well have, she thought, her breath quickening. She blinked, then peered closely at his solemn face, her gaze running over his rugged features as if he might vanish in a moment. *Smoke Eyes*. Only the folks she'd grown up with knew her by her Arapaho name.

With her heart in her throat, she lifted a hand and touched her fingers to his jaw. Black eyes, black hair. A hard, handsome face. She'd known a boy that fit that description, and had last seen him eleven years ago. Her mouth was suddenly dry, her throat aching as she opened her mouth to whisper one disbelieving word. "Zach?"

OFFICIAL RULES TO WINNERS CLASSIC SWEEPSTAKES

No Purchase necessary. To enter the sweepstakes follow instructions found elsewhere in this offer. You can also enter the sweepstakes by hand printing your name, address, city, state and zip code on a 3" x 5" piece of paper and mailing it to: Winners Classic Sweepstakes, P.O. Box 785, Gibbstown, NJ 08027. Mail each entry separately. Sweepstakes begins 12/1/91. Entries must be received by 6/1/93. Some presentations of this sweepstakes may feature a deadline for the Early Bird prize. If the offer you receive does, then to be eligible for the Early Bird prize your entry must be received according to the Early Bird date specified. Not responsible for lost, late, damaged, misdirected, illegible or postage due mail. Mechanically reproduced entries are not eligible. All entries become property of the sponsor and will not be returned.

Prize Selection/Validations: Winners will be selected in random drawings on or about 7/30/93, by VENTURA ASSOCIATES, INC., an independent judging organization whose decisions are final. Odds of winning are determined by total number of entries received. Circulation of this sweepstakes estimated not to exceed 200 million. Entrants need not be present to win. All prizes are guaranteed to be awarded and delivered to winners. Winners will be notified by mail and may be required to complete an affidavit of eligibility and release of liability which must be returned within 14 days of date of notification or alternate winners will be selected. Any guest of a trip winner will also be required to execute a release of liability. Any prize notification letter or any prize returned to a participating sponsor, Bantam Doubleday Dell Publishing Group, Inc., its participating divisions or subsidiaries, or VENTURA ASSOCIATES, INC. as undeliverable will be awarded to an alternate winner. Prizes are not transferable. No multiple prize winners except as may be necessary due to unavailability, in which case a prize of equal or greater value will be awarded. Prizes will be awarded approximately 90 days after the drawing. All taxes, automobile license and registration fees, if applicable, are the sole responsibility of the winners. Entry constitutes permission (except where prohibited) to use winners' names and likenesses for publicity purposes without further or other compensation.

Participation: This sweepstakes is open to residents of the United States and Canada, except for the province of Quebec. This sweepstakes is sponsored by Bantam Doubleday Dell Publishing Group, Inc. (BDD), 666 Fifth Avenue, New York, NY 10103. Versions of this sweepstakes with different graphics will be offered in conjunction with various solicitations or promotions by different subsidiaries and divisions of BDD. Employees and their families of BDD, its division, subsidiaries, advertising agencies, and VENTURA ASSOCIATES, INC., are not eligible.

Canadian residents, in order to win, must first correctly answer a time limited arithmetical skill testing question. Void in Quebec and wherever prohibited or restricted by law. Subject to all federal, state, local and provincial laws and regulations.

Prizes: The following values for prizes are determined by the manufacturers' suggested retail prices or by what these items are currently known to be selling for at the time this offer was published. Approximate retail values include handling and delivery of prizes. Estimated maximum retail value of prizes: 1 Grand Prize ($27,500 if merchandise or $25,000 Cash); 1 First Prize ($3,000); 5 Second Prizes ($400 each); 35 Third Prizes ($100 each); 1,000 Fourth Prizes ($9.00 each); 1 Early Bird Prize ($5,000); Total approximate maximum retail value is $50,000. Winners will have the option of selecting any prize offered at level won. Automobile winner must have a valid driver's license at the time the car is awarded. Trips are subject to space and departure availability. Certain black-out dates may apply. Travel must be completed within one year from the time the prize is awarded. Minors must be accompanied by an adult. Prizes won by minors will be awarded in the name of parent or legal guardian.

For a list of Major Prize Winners (available after 7/30/93): send a self-addressed, stamped envelope entirely separate from your entry to: Winners Classic Sweepstakes Winners, P.O. Box 825, Gibbstown, NJ 08027. Requests must be received by 6/1/93. DO NOT SEND ANY OTHER CORRESPONDENCE TO THIS P.O. BOX.

SWP 9/92

The Delaney Dynasty lives on in

The Delaney Christmas Carol

by Kay Hooper, Iris Johansen, & Fayrene Preston

Three of romantic fiction's best-loved authors present the changing face of Christmas spirit—past, present, and future—as they tell the story of three generations of Delaneys in love.

CHRISTMAS PAST by Iris Johansen

From the moment he first laid eyes on her, Kevin Delaney felt a curious attraction for the ragclad Gypsy beauty rummaging through the attic of his ranch at Killara. He didn't believe for a moment her talk of magic mirrors and second-sight, but something about Zara St. Cloud stirred his blood. Now, as Christmas draws near, a touch leads to a kiss and a gift of burning passion.

CHRISTMAS PRESENT by Fayrene Preston

Bria Delaney had been looking for Christmas ornaments in her mother's attic, when she saw him in the mirror for the first time—a stunningly handsome man with sky-blue eyes and red-gold hair. She had almost convinced herself he was only a dream when Kells Braxton arrived at Killara and led them both to a holiday wonderland of sensuous pleasure.

CHRISTMAS FUTURE by Kay Hooper

As the last of the Delaney men, Brett returned to Killara this Christmastime only to find it in the capable hands of his father's young and beautiful widow. Yet the closer he got to Cassie, the more Brett realized that the embers of their old love still burned and that all it would take was a look, a kiss, a caress, to turn their dormant passion into an inferno.

**The best in Women's Fiction from Bantam FANFARE.
On sale in November 1992**   AN 428 9/92

═FANFARE═

On Sale in November

RECKLESS
☐ 29315-X $5.50/6.50 in Canada
by Amanda Quick
New York Times bestselling author of
RENDEZVOUS and RAVISHED

THE DELANEY CHRISTMAS CAROL
☐ 29654-X $4.99/5.99 in Canada
by Kay Hooper, Iris Johansen, and Fayrene Preston

UNSUITABLE COMPANY
☐ 29712-0 $5.99/6.99 in Canada
by Judith Green

SARAH'S SIN
☐ 56050-6 $4.50//5.50 in Canada
by Tami Hoag
author of STILL WATERS and LUCKY'S LADY

SMOKE EYES
☐ 29501-2 $4.99/5.99 in Canada
by Maureen Reynolds
"A very HOT writer." --*Romantic Times*

Please send me the books I have checked above. I am enclosing $ _____ (add $2.50 to cover postage and handling). Send check or money order, no cash or C. O. D.'s please.

Name _____

Address _____

City/ State/ Zip _____

Send order to: Bantam Books, Dept. FN84, 2451 S. Wolf Rd., Des Plaines, IL 60018
Allow four to six weeks for delivery.
Prices and availability subject to change without notice.

Ask for these books at your local bookstore or use this page to order.

FN84 12/92

FANFARE

On Sale in December

THE TIGER PRINCE

☐ 29968-9 $5.50/6.50 in Canada
by Iris Johansen

Bantam's "Mistress of Romantic Fantasy"
author of THE GOLDEN BARBARIAN

LADY DEFIANT

☐ 29574-9 $4.99/5.99 in Canada
by Suzanne Robinson

Bestselling author of LADY GALLANT
and LADY HELLFIRE

"Lavish in atmosphere, rich in adventure, filled with suspense
and passion, LADY DEFIANT is a fitting sequel to
LADY GALLANT. Suzanne Robinson brilliantly captures the
era with all the intrigue, costume, drama, and romance that
readers adore."   --*Romantic Times*

PRIVATE SCANDALS

☐ 56053-0 $4.99//5.99 in Canada
by Christy Cohen

A stunning debut novel of friendship,
betrayal, and passionate romance

A LOVE FOR ALL TIME

☐ 29996-4 $4.50/5.50 in Canada
by Dorothy Garlock

One of Ms. Garlock's most beloved romances of all time

Ask for these books at your local bookstore or use this page to order.

☐ Please send me the books I have checked above. I am enclosing $ _____ (add $2.50
to cover postage and handling). Send check or money order, no cash or C. O. D.'s please.

Name _____

Address _____

City/ State/ Zip _____

Send order to: Bantam Books, Dept. FN85, 2451 S. Wolf Rd., Des Plaines, IL 60018
Allow four to six weeks for delivery.
Prices and availability subject to change without notice.

FN85 12/92